Dad Jokes

Justin Hunter

Planet Bizarro Press

Edited by Matthew A. Clarke

Proofread by Nick Clements

For William A. Hunter

Chapter 1

84′ Pontiac Fiero

"We wanted to get your brother a car for his sixteenth birthday, and a 1984 Pontiac Fiero 2M4 was the way to go. Hand me a 3/8 socket? I can't get this bastard off." The little girl reached into the immaculate toolbox and deftly plucked out the right size tool for her daddy. She placed it in his outstretched palm, his arm just visible from under the car. Her father shook the car with his efforts. His ample belly quivering and undulating as he worked. His jeans, ripped at one knee and oil-stained, wafted up the smell of sweat and axel grease. She watched him wriggle and jostle around and then become still. She stepped back just as he shoved himself out from under the car. The wheels on his creeper dug ruts in the concrete as his bulk crushed the wheels to immobility.

"Well, Fiona," he said. "I think we've got it!" His blonde hair was sweat pleated to his head. His beard almost covered his wide grin.

"Can we start it, Daddy?"

"Let's give her a rip." He carefully put his tools back into the toolbox. Fiona got into the car on the passenger's side. She'd loved the car ever since it was brought to them by tow truck all the way from Arizona. She touched the seats' old material and wondered how there were just two of them. She laughed when her daddy showed her how the engine was in the back instead of the front and laughed even harder when he showed her the spare tire under the hood.

From across the street, there came a loud popping sound. The inside of the front bay window of the neighbor's house was doused with crimson, staining the white curtains. Fiona saw it and opened her mouth to say something to her dad.

"Dad, the Smiths..."

"Aren't smart like your mother and I," her dad said, squishing his ample frame into the driver's seat. He closed the door and reached over to ruffle her hair. His hand caught for a second in a snarl, and he gently took it out. He remembered a promise to his wife that he would make sure she showered and dressed, but they got into the car right after breakfast, and the day seemed to melt away on them. He made a mental note to ensure she was scrubbed and ready before his wife got home from work.

"The Smiths bought their kid a 2005 F150 and that thing was in the scrapyard in a week." He fumbled in his pockets for the key. "Remember this, honey. Some day you may have kids of your own. Awesome old cars are going for cheap nowadays. Get yourself a good old car. One that's been taken care of, and you'll have it made. You can't work on new cars. They are all computers and fancy stuff. Your mother's VW broke down, and we're going to have to pay a mint to fix it. You need special tools and special computers and special training. Bah! Give me a wrench and a hammer, and you can fix anything on these old cars. This Pontiac is perfect, cheap, and will run another twenty years. It's got two seats, so he won't be able to pack this thing with all his hoodlum friends." He turned the key, and the engine turned over. They both slapped the dash, laughing and cheering. Fiona saw her father frown as he tapped the fuel gage stuck on E. Over the sound of the engine, she thought she could hear screaming, but maybe it was just children playing. Sometimes the kids got pretty loud, and an adult would come outside and tell them to shut up. But then there it was again. A woman's voice, loud, shrill, and long.

"Daddy?" Fiona said.

"Don't worry about it, honey," he said. He gave the gage a hard rap and shrugged. "I'll just have to check the wiring. Maybe the ground is off or something. No big deal."

The door to the house opened. Her mother poked her head into the garage. She was still wearing her nurse scrubs. Her eyes had dark circles under them, and her hair was knotted back in a ponytail.

"The house is a mess!" she said. "I've been working all day, and you've done nothing but work on that stupid car. Did you give Fiona a bath?"

"Not yet!" her father said, a brazen smile creasing his face. "We've been having a blast out here." Her mother looked away from them and out through the garage door. There were several people across the street at the Smith's house now. They were standing on the front lawn looking into the bay window. Fiona was sure she heard screaming now, from several voices.

"What's going on out there?" her mother said.

"I'll come in and clean up," her dad said. "I might not get to all of it. I've been working on this Pontiac's muffler all morning, and I'm EXHAUSTED!"

Her father's head exploded in a shower of blood and bits of brain and skull fragments. Fiona was washed in red. Her hands went up to her face and then into her tangled hair. She pulled one of her father's eyes out of her snarled hair. Her mother took a step down into the garage and slipped on the swath of gore. She hit her head on the steps and lay there moaning and holding onto the back of her head. Fiona got out of the car. She wandered out of the garage and into the street. Her neighbors were out in force. They were running about, fighting, and screaming. She held out her hands, but nobody seemed to notice her. She held up those hands toward the sun and gazed straight into that orb of light and fire. The rays glinted off the streaks of blood that covered her from head to toe. She stopped walking and sat down in the middle of the street. She allowed the black spots to dance in front of her vision. When it cleared, the first thing she saw was the Millers from a few houses down. Mrs. Miller had her hand over Mr. White's mouth. She held a finger to her own lips, demanding silence.

Chapter 2

Joyce & Chip Miller

Joyce Miller had her earbuds blasting away, hammering her eardrums in a way that would undoubtedly bog her golden years in deafness. That fact didn't cross her mind. She was thinking only of Ville Valo crooning a love song about suicide, death, and tearing appendages off of insects. She loved him. She knew she would just die if she ever saw him in person. She had no idea that he was pushing fifty years old. He was eternally the thin, pale, shadow-eyed, Goth god she saw on the cover of Razorblade Romance, her favorite album. Her cellphone buzzed next to her on the bed. She picked it up, saw it was her mom, and put it right back down again. She didn't know why her mother felt the need to call her all the time. Joyce remembered many conversations with her mom where she told her that texting was the best way to reach her. After she tried texting, she should try texting, texting, email, carrier pigeon, and if all that failed, call. Her mother told her that she would continue to do what she was doing and that she had to pick up her calls. Joyce had had enough. If her mom weren't going to go with the times,, she would be left behind. The phone kept ringing. Joyce turned the volume down on her cell and lay back down on her bed. She thought about the boys in her school. Did any of them look like

Ville? None came to mind. That was a hard no. Maybe she could pick up bits of Ville in one of them. Didn't Scott have his eyes? Maybe Phil had his pasty white skin. Maybe Joey had his thin, supple body. None had his fashion. None had his sensual voice.

Joyce opened up her eyes and sighed. She decided the boys in her town sucked, and she would die alone. She thought she might be hearing sirens when there came a loud thump against her wall. Two pictures fell to the floor, glass frames shattering. Joyce tore her earbuds out, vaulting out of bed and ripping open her door. She went to the door right next to her room. Stickers were slapped all over it. Some reading 'Fuck Off!' or 'Misfits' or 'Birds Aren't Real.' The rest were Keith Haring artworks; liquid stick figures with meat on their bones expressing various nothings.

She tried the doorknob, but it didn't turn. She called out, slamming an open palm on the door with rifle-quick slaps.

"Open up, asshole!" She kicked the door, feeling the whole house vibrate in response. Her toes ached. She ignored them. The door opened, and she stopped mid-slap before her hand touched that which she would never touch unless by unhappy accident. Her brother looked at her with annoyed hatred. He was shorter than she was and younger by three years. A beanie was pulled low to his eyes, brown hair billowing from underneath, the ends of which were snarled and unwashed. His skin was pock-marked with acne. A failure of a beard straggled over his chin.

"What?" he said.

"What the fuck, Chip?" Joyce said. "What was that noise? You knocked all my shit off my walls."

"Demon," Chip said. He pushed the door, but Joyce blocked it with her foot. She shoved it open, knocking her little brother back a step. She stepped into the room. Chip didn't try and stop her. He just idly scratched his pocked cheek, staring right at her.

His look didn't tell her anything, his face a blank, expressionless wall. Joyce looked around.

The room was much like she was used to seeing it. Joyce's best way of describing her brother's room was that it looked like a bomb went off right in its center. From the middle of the room and all the way toward the outer walls, it was spotlessly clean. From about a foot away from the walls, it was packed full of junk. Lying against the far wall and blocking the only window was Chip's bed. It was stood on its end and packed away like everything else.

Their parents had stopped arguing with him about it. They said that their job was to provide him with a bed. If he decided not to sleep in it, then that was his problem. The middle of the floor was open because her little brother was a little occult freak. There was no question that he was up to something in here. Around the clean part of the floor was a circle of salt. Joyce saw stacked Morton spheres in one corner of the room. Chip had drawn different shapes, sigils, and designs she wasn't familiar with in the circle. There were seven black candles in the circle. Four were up and burning. Three knocked over and snuffed, but she saw they were recently lit as there was a wisp of smoke coming from one of the wicks.

"What the fuck are you doing in here?" Joyce said.

"I'm summoning demons," Chip said.

"What demons?"

"Ones that will help me with killing dad."

"Freak," Joyce said. She moved to toe the circle of salt.

"I wouldn't do that," Chip said. "But it might be okay since the circle is already broken over there. That's how the other demon got out." Joyce brought her foot back and crossed her arms in front of her chest.

"Look," she said. "I don't really care what you're doing in here just as long as it doesn't knock all my shit down in my bedroom. Get a handle on it."

"Sorry," Chip said. "Can you get out of my room now?" Joyce took a step back but kept her body in the doorway, hesitating.

"Are you really trying to kill dad?" She said.

"Yeah," Chip said. He put a hand on the door to close it.

"Good," Joyce said. "Fucker's been gone for almost a week now. I don't think he's coming back at all this time." She took another step back and let Chip close the door. Joyce thought she heard a growl coming from within, but she shook her head. She turned to look down the hallway to the window by the stairs. She heard the sirens coming clearly now. Flashes of red and blue lights streaked through the window. Under the wail of the sirens, she heard the screams.

Chapter 3

Officer McFiggis's Shotgun

The shotgun in Officer McFiggis's police cruiser was having a magical day. He'd been McFiggis's gun for twelve long years, and every day he'd loved it, but today was something special. He remembered the day that he was bought. When the package opened, and the light finally shined, McFiggis held out his immense, hairy hands and picked him up. He looked him all over and caressed the etching on the stock. The shotgun leaked a little oil when that happened, but he was just a young gun then. Those types of things can happen to anyone. Officer McFiggis told him not to worry about it and that, in time, he would learn to hold his oil until it was time to fire. And fire he did. Those youthful days were spent at firing ranges. Shell after shell was pumped into him and expelled with fire and lead. Other officers would ask about him, and McFiggis would always tell them.

"He's alright."

And the shotgun knew it was so.

Those salad days weren't meant to last, and the shotgun knew that Officer McFiggis had others. He saw flashes of a snub-nosed .38 special he hid in a sleek, black hip holster. There was a silver 9mm he hid in his bedroom nightstand. There were many others in his basement, housed in giant black vaults and neatly set inside and surrounded with cases and cases of bullets of all different sizes. Officer McFiggis was a man with many guns, but the shotgun knew that they didn't mean anything to him. They were one-night stands. They were his weekend shooters. They were placed and forgotten. Only the shotgun was his everyday partner. There were some days that the shotgun felt a tinge of jealousy, but more often than not, he felt great empathy for the other guns. To only feel the touch of your lover once or twice in a lifetime must have been the greatest torture. Sure, their romance wasn't what it used to be. Officer McFiggis cleaned him once a week like clockwork on Saturday afternoons after Wheel of Fortune. They did it in the same bed, in the same comfortable way. There was not much excitement in it anymore, but there was comfort in the routine.

But today...today he was flying.

For twelve years, they'd been partners. Every morning he would pick up the shotgun and bring it out to his police cruiser, stick it into place, and go about his work. They would drive the street together. Officer McFiggis would sometimes have to leave the car to do some work, but his shotgun would wait patiently, and he always came back. At the end of the day, Officer McFiggis would take the shotgun out of the cruiser and place it on the rack in the bedroom right over his hunting bow.

The shotgun was never jealous of the hunting bow. He knew McFiggis didn't swing that way.

But today was different. There was the calling over the walkie-talkie. McFiggis sounded different as he answered dispatch. His growly voice was higher and halting. The shotgun was used to such a commanding tone that he had to take a peek to make sure there wasn't someone else in the car. Their siren was blaring. The car was moving quickly through the streets of the town. The shotgun saw people running, but he wasn't exactly sure what they were running from. There didn't seem to be any real direction to their running. They were just fleeing, but from what? The shotgun saw blood splatters on the runners' clothing. It was on their faces and hair. He thought that maybe they had done something wrong and were running away from what they had done. But then they were gathering and holding each other. He saw them screaming in each other's arms. He saw them coming together in protection and fear.

The car pulled up to a curb, and Officer McFiggis opened the door and stopped. The shotgun was used to the grunt-out-close regular movements of his beloved, but this time he paused. Then he reached in and grabbed him by the barrel, and pulled him free. He was gripping him tightly and staring over the top of his car. There was a man on the ground. His body was face-down and stopped at the neck. Beyond that was a cascade of blood and bits of gore. It was a deconstruction of a human head. A million-piece jigsaw puzzle drenched in red liquid. Officer McFiggis pumped the shotgun, and he became hard. The shell cocked right into position.

Shoot me, McFiggis. The shotgun thought. *Pull that trigger and watch me explode hot lead all over. I'm alive. I'm out of the car, and I'm alive! I feel so young and free! Pull that trigger and watch me explode, then pump me again. I won't mind. All you want, Officer McFiggis, I will give you all you want.*

McFiggis screamed out an order, waited, and nobody answered him. He ran up to the body and swore. He looked all around, swinging the shotgun in every direction. He was ready to kill the first malevolent thing he saw. Over to the left of him was another body. He moved toward it, and it looked to be the same type of death. Exploded head. Is that what the guys in the lab would call it? Exploded head? He wondered what kind of weapon could do that to somebody. The head was gone. It wasn't the first time Officer McFiggis saw someone without a head, but it wasn't like he saw it a lot. This was a small town with small-town people having small-town problems. And there wasn't any damage to the clothing at the neck. No burn marks. No shredding. It was like the head had just popped.

Officer McFiggis moved back to the patrol car. He looked down at his shotgun. He could have sworn the thing quivered. He shook his head and got on the radio.

"What the fuck is going on, dispatch?" he asked.

"Multiple deaths," the voice came over the radio. "Non-stop emergency calls. People aren't making sense, Dan. They say people are just dying."

"Where do you need me?"

"We're sending ambulances. Call in with body sightings. Start interviewing witnesses."

"Witnesses? Who?"

"I think you could talk to just about anybody," Dispatch said. "It's like we're under siege. Hold on."

The shotgun felt his stock nestling against Officer McFiggis's hip. The chambered shell was so firm and long that it almost hurt, but it was a perfect sort of hurt. Sometimes he didn't feel whole unless his chamber was full. He kept thinking about his trigger and how much he wanted it to be pulled, but he tried to stop himself. He wanted to be patient and understanding. He tried remembering that sometimes the build-up was better than the release.

McFiggis stepped away from the cruiser when he saw a woman running toward him. She had long auburn hair and was wearing a yellow t-shirt and jeans. She was covered in blood.

"Jenny?" Officer McFiggis said, "what's going on?" She nearly crashed into him, grabbing him by the shirt and pulling him close to her. Her eyes were wide. She spat as she spoke.

"Gary is dead!" she said, pulling at him with each uttered syllable. "He's dead!"

"What happened? Are you hurt?"

"This isn't my blood! It's Gary's!"

"Where is he?"

"Back at the store. Help me." She pulled at him, and he followed at a trot. His heavy legs pounded on the asphalt while hers ran lightly like a deer. McFiggis looked down at his uniform and the blood stains Jenny had left on him. He spoke to her while they ran.

"What happened to him?"

"I don't know," Jenny said. "We were just talking, and then all of a sudden his head exploded."

"Was he shot? Was it a bomb?"

"His head just fucking exploded! It's like everybody is dying all at once."

"Are you sure you don't know how he died?"

"Are you just as stupid as you were in high school?" Jenny said, turning her face and shrieking her anger at him. "His head is gone! Help me."

"I'll help you, Jenny," Officer McFiggis replied. "Just lead the way."

'Shoot. Shoot. Shoot. Shoot. Shoot-shoot-shoot-shoot-shoot,' thought the shotgun.

Officer McFiggis knew where they were going. Jenny and Gary owned a Hardware store down on Main Street. It was dying a slow death as there was a Lowes and a Home Depot just one county over. The siphoning of their business by their big-box competitors was increasing every year as they increased their service offerings. Their prices were at least twenty percent lower than Jenny's store, and they had more options. The only thing keeping them alive was if people were too lazy to make the fifteen-minute drive to the chain stores. But man, McFiggis thought, twenty percent lower prices beats laziness in most people.

Jenny opened the door to her store with McFiggis entering close behind. He was breathing heavily, and beads of sweat formed on his forehead. He leaned forward and took a deep breath. On the floor in front of them was Gary. His head was indeed everywhere, splattering the electric outlet parts section with blood. Jenny was screaming.

"Call an ambulance!"

"They're on the way," McFiggis said. "They're swamped. I don't know when they'll get here. I have to report it." McFiggis thought a hearse would be a better option than an ambulance, but he didn't say it. The shotgun saw the dead body and thought he could do a better job than that. Jenny dropped to her knees beside her husband's body. She wept and tried pulling him onto her lap.

"You have to leave him, Jenny," McFiggis said.

"He's all I have," Jenny said. "This place is going under. He's all I have left. I have nothing without him." Officer McFiggis put his hand on her shoulder, giving it a reassuring pat.

"You have friends here," McFiggis said. "I'm so sorry, Jenny."

Jenny ran a finger through a thick gob of blood on the floor. She pushed a bit of brain matter aside.

"You and I," she said. "We used to be friends. Do you remember?"

"I do," McFiggis said. "I was on the football team. Left Tackle. You were a cheerleader."

"You were always after me in those days. Remember what you used to tell me?"

"I do," Mcfiggis put the shotgun over his shoulder. He smiled. Jenny put a bloody finger to her lips and sucked it. "I told you that one day I'd be your man."

"So?" Jenny said. "Will you be my man today?" She got up off the floor and wiped her hands on her jeans. She went behind the counter. McFiggis gave a quizzical look and took his walkie-talkie off his uniform strap.

"I've got a body here at J & G Hardware on Main Street. Send an ambulance."

"Got you," Dispatch answered. "It's going to be a bit. Crazy out there. Stay safe."

"Thanks."

Jenny reached under the cash counter and took out a Heritage Arms .44 Magnum. McFiggis smiled.

"Now, Jenny, what are you going to do with that? Put that down, and let's get you out of here."

"Are you going to be my man?" Jenny said. She checked the gun to make sure it was loaded and looked up at McFiggis. Her facial features were drawn. Her eyes seemed to look right through him.

"Put it down, Jenny."

"Do you remember back after that game in '98? You guys just won against West High and were crowding around at mid-field. I ran out with the other cheerleaders, and we were all yelling and jumping and so happy. You grabbed me and kissed me."

"I remember," McFiggis said. "You slapped me a good one." Jenny laughed.

"I did. Even left a couple of scratches on your face, if I remember right."

"I deserved it. But I had a thing for you back then. I had to take my shot. The moment felt right."

"You want to take a shot now?" Jenny tapped the magnum on the counter.

"Don't know what you're talking about, and I don't think I want to. Put that gun down, and let's go. We can talk about old times in the car."

"You going to try and kiss me again?"

"No," McFiggis said, pulling his features into a good-natured grin. "Old times and old days. I'm not a teenager anymore. I'm just a cop, and we've got an emergency. I want to keep you safe. Can't you hear the sirens? The screams?"

"I hear them," Jenny said. "Can't help it. The world seems to be falling apart right before our eyes. But my world has been dying for a while now. The store is shit. I thought it was going to be a slow death, but now with Gary gone, it's all over. There's no way I can run this place by myself. No money to hire any help. In some ways, it's a good thing. It's easier to see something explode than to watch it slowly die." She raised the gun, pointing it at McFiggis. The officer pulled his shotgun down to his hip. His finger was on the trigger.

"Put the fucking gun down, Jenny."

"I don't think so. I think I'm done."

Oh, fuck yes, shoot.

Jenny pulled back the hammer on the gun. Mcfiggis tightened his finger on the trigger. He knew the weapon. He knew at just what moment it would fire. A tiny little bit more pressure on the trigger, and Jenny would be a mess of pulp.

"Ever hear of suicide by cop?" Jenny said.

"Don't make me live with that," McFiggis said. "Don't make me do it."

A little more. Yes. Yes. Yes. Just a little more. I'm about to burst. I'm gonna burst!

"Do you want to kiss me?" Jenny said.

"Put the gun down!"

Do it. Do it. Do it. Do it.

McFiggis saw her trigger finger tremble. It was enough. He pulled the trigger, and the shotgun blast rocked the little hardware store. McFiggis felt his eardrums flex. His vision wavered and he lost all hearing. He fell backward onto the floor and realized he had been grazed in the arm by her bullet. He looked behind him and saw a smoking hole in a piece of plywood. A trickling of blood was seeping down his arm from the wound. His hearing came back, and he looked for Jenny. She was lying behind the cash counter. Her chest was a ripped mess. Her face was already turning gray. There was no life in her eyes. McFiggis leaned over on the cash counter and began to cry.

The shotgun was beside himself with joy. He knew that McFiggis was a man, but he didn't know how much of a man! It was his first manage-a-trois, and he wanted more of it. He kind of wished that the officer had spoken to him beforehand about bringing another person into their lovemaking, but it turned out okay. He knew he just had to trust McFiggis, and everything would be okay. He could see the lower half of Jenny's body from where McFiggis laid him down. She wasn't moving anymore. The shotgun was reeling from actually cumming inside someone. Before this, he had to spend his blasts into a target or wall. This was something else entirely. He wondered if she would get up and be up to another blast or two.

Chapter 4

Joyce Miller & the Asshole Boyfriend

Joyce didn't think that she would be able to make her date tonight. The National Guard had quarantined their town and imposed strict curfews. No person was to be out and about after nine in the evening. People were not allowed to gather outside of their jobs or families. Joyce had never seen anyone from the military before. At least not one that wasn't old. There were Vietnam veterans, but Joyce always felt weird about how they were celebrated. There was old Mr. Frank, who she knew was a soldier in the Vietnam War. He had tanned and spotty skin. His head was barely hanging onto thin wisps of white hair. He used to sit on the bench of the city bus stop, which was the same stop used by her school bus.

"I didn't do much fighting during the war," Old Mr. Frank said. "There wasn't to be any jungle slogging for me. No crawling into underground tunnels searching out enemies. No burning villages. No!"

"What did you do?" Joyce asked him. She learned quickly from her past experiences with Mr. Frank that you must keep the conversation on point. If it strayed, there was no guessing what the man might talk about, but it was usually a tirade of vulgarity mixed with racist propaganda.

"The brass asked our group when we came in if any of us knew how to cut hair, and I raised my hand. That kept me out of all the shit. I spent the war knee-deep in hippie hair."

"So you were a barber before the war?"

"Hell no!" Mr. Frank said. "But I wasn't a stupid dipshit either. I had no idea how to give a man a haircut, but I raised my hand all the same. For the life of me, I still can't understand why none of the others did. It was an obvious way to keep a gun out of my hand, and I took it. I would have raised my hand if they'd asked if any of us was a classically trained ballerina. I didn't kill anybody or do anything in the war, but when I came home, there was nothing but trouble." Their conversations were always about the war and always ended in his homecoming.

"What happened?" she said.

"It was a Sunday, and I went right to church," Old Mr. Frank said. "My Sunday school teachers, Violet and Summer, took one look at me and called me a baby killer. They didn't want nothing to do with me. I was scorned by them and so many others that I didn't bother going anymore. It was like that everywhere. At the grocery store, bar, you name it. I was reviled. Nowadays, they got their parades and their politicians talking about how wonderful we who served in the military are. The only problem is that there aren't any WWII veterans left, so they try and parade us out there like we mean something. It's all horseshit. They prop us up there and say how much they love us, but it's all shit."

Now the military was crawling everywhere outside. She saw them patrolling and collecting the dead. She saw reports on her cell phone showing blockades at the roads and waterfronts. She saw videos of many tents put up for scientists to conduct interviews and experiments to try and figure out what was going on. So what did this mean for her date? She wasn't sure. Marky wasn't a bad boyfriend to her, but he wasn't that great either. She thought about how she met him through some mutual friends at the mall where he worked at Hot Topic. He had box-dyed black hair, black eyeshadow, and a completely black wardrobe. He wasn't her boyfriend per se, more like a friend that she dated. At least that's how she saw it. She didn't know how Marky saw their relationship since she never asked him directly. Sometimes a whole week would pass without them speaking, but he didn't seem to mind that either. Joyce didn't know anything that really rankled him except once she asked about his name, and he told her he was named Marky after Mark Wahlberg's band Marky Mark and the Funky Bunch. Joyce started singing Good Vibrations, and he cut her off. Joyce wondered why he went by 'Marky' if he was so embarrassed by it.

She sent Marky a text asking if he was still showing up, and he responded with a thumbs-up emoji.

"Okay..." she said. There was a thump on the wall, but Joyce didn't move. She'd gotten used to all sorts of noises coming from Chip's room and stopped concerning herself about them. She rechecked her phone, but there were no updates. Marky was two hours late, and she was about to send him a scathing text when there was a clattering at her window. She looked up to see Marky. He waved to her, and she opened up the window.

"What the fuck are you doing?" She asked.

"I couldn't go to your front door," Marky said. "There's soldiers out there. It's past curfew."

"You should have come sooner."

"Couldn't," Marky said. He pointed inside. "Can I come in?" Joyce stepped aside and let Marky climb through. She closed her window.

"I hope you didn't break anything getting up here."

"No. It was easy. Stood on the porch rail and pulled up at the roofline. It's way too easy to get up to your room."

"I hope my mom didn't see you."

"She's not here. Her car is gone."

"I'm not surprised," Joyce said. Marky sat down on her bed, taking his phone out of his pocket and setting it next to him. Joyce turned on some music at her computer. Robert Smith began singing about photographs. "She's always leaving now and not telling me. What is she doing out after curfew anyway?"

"Beats me." Marky shrugged. "Why don't you sit down with me here on the bed? I've missed you." Joyce sat, and Marky put his arm around her shoulder, pulling her in for a kiss. She let him kiss her, but pushed him back after a mere second.

"I thought we were going out?" Joyce said, putting her hand on his thigh.

"We could, but I'm not sure where it is we can go. The movie theater will be closed. The curfew closes everything. Can't drive anywhere. If you can think of something, we'll go."

"I guess you're right," Joyce said. "But I'm too bored with staying here."

"There are things we can do to pass the time." Marky leaned in for another kiss. This time Joyce kissed him back. His breath smelled like blueberry vape with a hint of garlic. She wondered if he would be upset if she offered him an Altoid. He put his hand up under her shirt and pinched her nipple through her bra. She shoved him away.

"What the fuck, Marky."

"What the fuck? I was just having fun."

"Why the fuck would I want you to pinch my nipple?"

"I like your nipples," Marky said. "I don't know. I just thought we could take things to the next level."

"Well, you thought wrong." Joyce stood up and adjusted her shirt. Marky flopped backward on the bed. He let his arms fall to the sides.

"You know this is why I don't call you," Marky said. "I thought we could have a good time, but you're never in the mood. I think there's something wrong with you."

"There's nothing wrong with me," Joyce said, thinking about what she had nearby she could throw at his head. "Just because I won't put out doesn't mean something's wrong with me. You are such an asshole. I think you should leave." Marky sat up and held his arms out to her.

"I am an asshole," Marky said. "Look, I'm sorry. I don't know why I said that."

"Get the fuck out!"

"Just wait a minute. Don't make me go. Let's talk about this."

There was a knock at the door. Joyce was both afraid and relieved that it might be her mom. It would be nice to let her mom kick Marky out, but she was afraid that her mom would be angry with her for having him in her room. Her dad's rule was that boys weren't allowed in her room with the door closed. Her mother didn't want boys in her life at all.

Joyce answered the door and saw Chip. He was staring up at her. A scratch on his cheek was leaking a little blood. His Misfits t-shirt was drenched in sweat and clinging to his body.

"You okay? I heard yelling," Chip said, pushing his sweaty hair out of his eyes.

"I'm okay," Joyce said.

"Well, look who's here," Marky said, standing and walking over. "What's up, little guy?" Joyce left the doorway and went back over to the bed.

"Hello," Chip said.

"Are you working out or something?" Marky said. "Why are you so sweaty? You having a marathon whacking-off session over there?" Marky's phone buzzed on the bed. Joyce glanced at it.

"I'm trying to get the demons to remove the curse," Chip said.

"Ooooooh, how's that going?" Marky said.

"Not great."

"Well, you hang in there, little dude. I'm sure you'll banish all those demons to World of Warcraft or whatever," Marky said, looking back at Joyce, who was holding his phone in her hands.

"Who is Lenore?" Joyce said. "Lenore from school?"

"I don't know what you're talking about," Marky said.

"Someone named Lenore just texted you asking you to come over," Joyce said. "You have another girlfriend?" There was a thump on the wall that shook the whole house. Chip rolled his eyes and went back to his room.

"I don't have ANY girlfriend," Marky said. "You aren't my girlfriend. Lenore isn't my girlfriend. Nobody owns me."

"Are you fucking Lenore? Is that why you see her?"

"Lenore isn't a prude like you are." Joyce threw the phone at his head. He caught it deftly and checked his messages.

"We're done," Joyce said. "Just go."

"Fine," Marky said. "Sound like she really wants to see me anyway. Call me if you ever change your mind and want to have some real-life experience."

"Get out."

"Okay," Marky said. "I am sorry for being a dick." He stepped to the window and opened it.

"You have a small dick," Joyce said.

"I had a girlfriend once who said nothing was wrong with having a small dick. I told her that was true, but I still wished she didn't have one!" Marky said. His laughter turned into a grimace. He let go of the window and turned to Joyce. His eyes were so wide they looked like they were about to pop out. His lips moved, but no words were coming out. His head exploded, turning half the room into a midnight abattoir. Joyce screamed and sat down on her blood-soaked carpet. Chip opened her bedroom door, looked inside, and then left, closing the door behind him. Joyce was crying and holding her head in her hands. The buzz of a cell phone permeated the palpable silence of the room. She got up off the floor and went to Marky's body. She reached into his pocket and took out his phone. It was Lenore calling. She answered.

"Hello," Joyce said.

"Who is this?" Lenore said. Joyce heard her voice and knew her from school.

"This is Joyce. I have Marky's phone."

"I knew he was sleeping around on me," Lenore said. "Tell that fucker that we're done. And we are going to talk about this at school. I should kick your fucking..."

"Lenore, shut up a minute," Joyce said. "What did you have to talk to him about?"

"None of your fucking business, slut."

"He was cheating on us," Joyce said, and there was a moment of silence on the other line. Then sobbing as Lenore lost all composure.

"Fuck him," Lenore said. "Fuck him!" Joyce looked around at the gore fest that used to be her room.

"Yeah, fuck him," she said. She pushed a piece of Marky's brain with her toe as she said comforting words to the now-wailing Lenore over the cell phone.

Chapter 5
Mr. Miller

Mr. Miller had a headache. Prone to migraines, he knew this one would be a particularly bad episode. He took two Tylenol extra-strength capsules and lay down on the fetid couch at the Motel Sunnyside fifty miles down Highway 61 in Missouri. The motel was as disgusting as it was cheap. For thirty-five bucks, it was his haven until he hit the road for as long as he could keep his eyes open the next day. The sleepy clerk took cash and handed him an oily key. The room was just as he thought it would be. Musty carpet, lumpy bed, unclean bathroom, scurrying roaches, and a sink with a dripping tap greeted him upon entry. He put his suitcase down on the floor and immediately lay down on the couch. The couch was an extra touch to the room that he hadn't expected. Although, the extra comfort was as dingy as everything else. A velvet Elvis painting hung above the bed, which made him smile. A relic like that would fetch a nice price at a hipster retro thrift shop, but here it hung, forgotten. A thing probably worth more than everything else in the room put together.

"Shit," Mr. Miller said, rubbing his temples with his fingers clockwise. He opened his eyes and saw black dots dancing in his vision. Yes, he thought, this was going to be a bad one.

The parking lot of this dubious establishment had only a couple trucks parked, which would make his newer model Honda stand out, but he wasn't worried. It wasn't like he'd broken any law or thought that anyone would be looking for him, let alone at a place like this. He'd left his family, again, and this time he didn't figure on coming back. His cell phone had one text from his wife asking where he was, but that was all. He knew he'd given Mrs. Miller a tough time over the years, and she was fairly helpless to control his decisions and actions. Or maybe she was just resigned to them or didn't want to put any useless effort into trying to bring him back. Whatever it was, it was fine with him.

He took two more Tylenol and sat up, thinking that a shower might help, or maybe some food. He'd asked the motel clerk about restaurants nearby.

"Nothing around here like that," he said. "Another twenty miles or so, and you'll find something, but not here. The only place you can get food is the Raging Stallion next door."

"The strip club?"

"Best one around," the clerk said with a leer. "Last stop for some of these ladies. Desperate and willing."

"I'm not interested in that," Mr. Miller said. "I just want some food."

"They give a buffet for customers from five until eight," the clerk said. "It's not great, but it's food. Remember, if you bring a lady back with you, the room's price goes up to fifty. It's thirty-five for one person, not two."

"I'll remember."

"See that you do," the clerk said. He turned back to his cell phone. He was watching The Office with the sound turned all the way up. Mr. Miller didn't say goodbye before leaving. As he was sitting up in his bed, his stomach growled, and he made his decision. He took a suitcoat out of his luggage and put it on, brushed his teeth, and combed his hair. He wasn't too sure why he was trying to look nice, but he'd never been to a strip club before and felt better getting tidy. He walked out of his room and locked the door. He looked around the parking lot, but nobody was there. He shook the keys in his hand and looked at the office. Worried that there must be another set of keys and that his stuff would be stolen before he got back, but deciding there was nothing to do about it, he went toward the club.

It was a short walk. Right across the parking lot, actually, sharing the parking lot of the motel. It was a wood-sided building, one story, painted all in black with what looked like flat house paint. A white-painted horse reared on its back legs by the door. The roof was corrugated metal, painted with silver-toned roofing tar. The sign was painted in pink and said 'Ragging Stallions.' A tire-shaped bald man wearing a black t-shirt and jeans came out the front door carrying a trash bag. He brought it to the dumpster and tossed it in. He returned to the front door, lit a cigarette, and took a long drag. He gestured to Mr. Miller with the cigarette.

"Come on in," he said. "They won't bite you."

"I heard you have food in there."

"There's a buffet for customers," the man said. "I work here. You pay a five-dollar cover charge at the door, and you can go in there and duck in."

"And there's strippers?" Mr. Miller said. The man put his cigarette in his mouth and gave him a side glance.

"Dancers," he said, letting a stream of smoke run out his nostrils. "We call them dancers here."

"Sorry," Mr. Miller said. The man waited a moment and then slapped Mr. Miller hard in the stomach. He was belly laughing. The cigarette jumped up and down between his lips.

"Just fucking with you, man! Of course we've got strippers in there. Well, one stripper now. It's a little early for the rest."

Mr. Miller rubbed his stomach. The man frowned. "I was just fucking with you. Have a sense of humor."

"You hit me." Mr. Miller felt like he was going to vomit.

"You're soft," the man said. "Don't see much of your type here. Looks like you're an office guy. Desk, and all of that shit. It's not like it's my fault your stomach is as hard as a marshmallow."

"I'm sorry."

"Twice you're sorry," the man said. "Don't be such a wimpy shit. You're going to give me five bucks, and then you're going to walk in there like you're the cock in the henhouse. Head up. Chin up. Be a fucking man, for Christ's sakes." Mr. Miller took a ten out of his wallet and handed it over.

"I don't have any change," the man said.

"Don't worry about it," Mr. Miller said. The man waved him to the door.

"I'm going to finish my cigarette. You get on in there cock-of-the-walk."

"Thanks," Mr. Miller said. The man rolled his eyes and grunted. He lit another cigarette off the first one. Mr. Miller went to the door and pulled it open. Smells of sweat, cigarettes, and dusty carpet hit him broadly. The meager lighting was directed at the stage where a topless middle-aged woman danced to Rio by Duran Duran. There was a bartender, dusky-skinned and muscled. He was wiping off a glass with a stained towel. Next to the bar was a small DJ setup. They were the only ones in the place. The woman nodded to Mr. Miller and kept on dancing. Mr. Miller nodded back.

"Hello," he said. "I'm just here for the food." The woman frowned at him and did the splits. She got back up rather ungracefully. The bartender called to him.

"Want a drink?"

"Yes," Mr. Miller said. "And some food. Miller Lite, please." The bartender took a bottle out from the small fridge behind him, untwisted the cap with his fingers, and put it in front of Mr. Miller.

"Four bucks," he said.

"That's a lot for a beer."

"Special is a buck for a Pabst. You can drink those after this one if you're feeling thrifty."

"I'll stick with this," Mr. Miller replied. "Where can I find the food?"

"Over there, next to the stage. There's a table where you can fix yourself up a plate. Sandwiches and some chips. I put a veggie tray out there as well, but I usually go home with that for leftovers." Mr. Miller put a twenty on the counter.

"Keep this for my tab," he said. The bartender nodded and tacked the twenty to a cork board over the register. Mr. Miller took his beer over to the folding table next to the stage. The table had a thin layer of fake green leather and was worn at the edges. There were two loaves of bread; white and wheat, some sandwich meat, and a head of lettuce. Two big bags of Ruffles Potato Chips and a small veggie tray finished up the ensemble. Mr. Miller picked up a thin paper plate and began gathering food. The stripper walked over to him and squatted down. The stage was at the perfect height so that when she squatted, Mr. Miller got a good look at her ponderous breasts. He reddened.

"I'm sorry," he said. "I'm just here for the food."

"You can still spare a little cash," she said. "Even if you're not interested, which I doubt. All men are interested." Mr. Miller took out a ten-dollar bill from his wallet, the last of his cash, and handed it to her. She took it and walked away from him.

"I'm married," he said. A few chips fell off his plate and onto the table.

"So am I," she said. "Stop being a fucking idiot." Mr. Miller sure felt like an idiot as he went back to the bar, sat down, and began eating. He found the food filling and pleasant enough. He tapped his shirt pocket and frowned. The bartender laughed.

"You're looking for invisible cigarettes?"

"I am," Mr. Miller said.

"I do that all the time. How long since you quit?"

"Four years," Mr. Miller said around a mouthful of sandwich. "Still have the want of one all the time."

"It's this place," the bartender said. "There's not many places left that allow smoking. This place reeks of it. I quit two weeks ago, but I know I'll start up again. I quit all the time. It never lasts." The bartender gave him another Miller Lite. Mr. Miller took a bite of chips. The stripper sat down next to him at the bar. She was wearing a tattered white bathrobe over her body.

"Give me a shot," she said, and the bartender poured her a rail vodka. She held the glass out to Mr. Miller. "Cheers."

"Cheers," Mr. Miller said, clinking his bottle against her glass. They drank. "So...are you all done then?"

"No," she said. "I have to dance for fifteen minutes at opening. If nobody's here for me, then I get to sit down. This place won't pick up for another few hours."

"So you get a lot of people here?"

"Druggies, drunks, or truckers," she said. "We call it the holy trinity here. Most of the truckers are drunks and druggies. They take all these uppers to stay awake behind the wheel and have to get drunk to fall asleep."

"How long have you been here?"

"A couple weeks," she said, taking out a pack of Marlboro Reds from her pocket. She shook two out and handed one to Mr. Miller. The bartender smirked.

"He's quit," he said.

"No, he hasn't," the stripper said. "Don't make me smoke alone." She lit her cigarette and held the lighter out. Mr. Miller lit his, inhaled, and immediately everything in the world was better.

"I'm Heidi," she said.

"Steven Miller."

"I answered three questions from you," Heidi said, holding out her shot glass so the bartender could fill it up. "Now it's your turn. You'll be honest with me, or I'll fold you in half, unzip my stomach, and feed you inside."

Mr. Miller thought she was extraordinary. "Go ahead," he said. "Shoot."

Chapter 6

Scientist Bob

The canvas tent was set up right before the Madison Bridge in an empty parking lot. Surrounding the tent was chain metal fencing topped with barbed wire. Soldiers from the National guard milled about outside, some on duty, some unsure what their duty was. Inside the tent were scientists and their assistants. Tarps were hung from the tent ceiling to cordon off rooms filled with computers, lab equipment, and beds for the sick. But there weren't any sick. Scientist Bob had only the dead to work with.

Scientist Bob had been there for a week, spending his nights at Radisson and his days in the tent. He hated both places equally. He missed his wife and wondered why he hadn't retired yet so that he could spend time with her and visit his beloved grandchildren. He scratched his bald head, which showed several spots that were likely to become cancer one day. His eyes squinted behind Coke bottle glasses. All the hair that left his head held rank over all other areas of his body. He looked to be covered in thick white fur up to his neck. He was stooped over the headless body of a man. Medical tweezers snapped in his hand as he pecked at a morsel of flesh in the dead man's neck.

His cell phone rang, and he put the tweezers down and answered the call.

"Yes, sir?"

"Fuck that 'sir' nonsense and tell me what's going on there. I can't have a problem without a solution- or at least an idea of what the problem is. The press is eating me alive. Not to mention the President. He's calling me nearly every hour." Scientist Bob and the Colonel had been longtime friends since their time in Afghanistan during a curious outbreak of plague in the early 2000s. There was no friendship in his voice now.

"I wish I could tell you what's going on. I still don't know. We are conducting every sort of test we can think of."

"Well, you must know something," the Colonel said. "What do you know?"

"This event is happening to males only. It seems indiscriminate of age, but the youngest to die was fifteen years old. We've tested the bodies, and we're finding no correlation between any found drugs or medical history. We've conducted interviews with surviving men in the town, and interestingly, they are all without children."

"So having a child causes their heads to explode?"

"There may be some hormonal changes that happen to a man when he becomes a father, but nothing that would make a person's head explode. There's a loss of testosterone and prolactin, vasopressin, and oxytocin gain. That's it."

"Are there any other correlations?"

"None that come to mind." Scientist Bob picked up his tweezers and began tearing at the body's severed neck.

"So dads in this town are spontaneously combusting, and there's nothing we can do, and we don't know why. That's just great."

"They aren't combusting. That would mean fire, and there's no sign of that here. We have to do more tests, is all. I'm sure we will figure this out soon. Have no fear...sir."

"Fuck off, Bob."

"Goodbye." Scientist Bob ended the call and put the phone down on the table. He put a piece of neck meat on a slide and brought it over to a microscope. He began humming off-key and peered closely through the lens.

"I'll figure out what's going on," Scientist Bob said aloud to nobody. "I don't know why he's so upset. It's nothing to lose your head over."

Scientist Bob chuckled to himself. His head exploded.

Chapter 7

Mrs. Miller

Mrs. Miller walked into the Rusty Nail. She picked the dive bar because it was at the end of Main Street, the farthest from anywhere anyone reputable would hang out. Wood paneling festooned with neon signs covered every space of open wall. It hurt her eyes to look at them, and from the downcast eyes of the other patrons, she expected it hurt theirs too. She wondered what kind of a bar wanted its customers to always look down. She took a seat at the only booth in the back. The fake leather, dyed a harsh red, squelched as she sat. The bartender came from around the bar and plonked a glass ashtray in front of her.

"What do you want, Mrs. Miller?"

"Give me a seven and seven, Gavin," she said, taking a pack of menthol Kools out of her handbag and setting the rumpled pack on the table.

"Are you starting a tab?" Gavin asked. She handed him a twenty, and he took it behind the bar. He brought back two drinks and put them in front of her, saying that he didn't want to keep coming back repeatedly. Mrs. Miller looked around the bar, noticing a few people she knew. She noted the absence of women and downed her first drink with one gulp. Someone put Meatloaf on the jukebox. She fucking loved Meatloaf.

"I fucking love Meatloaf," she said.

"Hell yeah!" That was Horace Green. Mrs. Miller knew him by his bald head, which reflected the blue light from the Lowenbrau neon sign over his head. He got up from the bar and walked over to her.

"Are you staring at my head?" he said.

"Yes," Mrs. Miller said. "I can't help it, Horace. If you're bald, then just shave the whole fucking thing. That horseshoe of hair above your ears makes you look like a monk."

"Can I sit down?" he said.

"Go ahead," Mrs. Miller said, waving her hand over the nearly empty booth.

"So, what are you doing here so early?" Mr. Green said. "Don't usually see you until evening. Things all right at home?"

"Whoa, are we friends or something? I thought we were nodding acquaintances. Why would I want to tell you about my personal life?"

"I have a face you can trust." Horace Green took a drink of beer and called for a couple of shots. "You don't have to tell me shit, but you're going to do a shot with me. I'm celebrating a sale."

"Congrats," Mrs. Miller said. "What do you sell again?"

"Medical supplies. Mostly bags and tubing for pump feeders. You don't have to act interested. Everything about the job is boring except for the money. I got the Mercy Hospital account. The fucking white whale, and it's all mine. Drink up." The bartender poured two shots of Old Crow whiskey and left the bottle on the table.

"Here's to people being so fucked up they eat through a belly tube," Mrs. Miller said. She took her shot and slammed the glass upside down on the table. Horace Green grimaced and drank down his shot.

"It sounds kind of shitty when you say it like that," he said. Mrs. Miller patted his hand.

"Don't worry. We're all going to end up eating through a tube, shitting ourselves, and full of weeping bed sores in the end." Horace turned her shot glass up and filled it. "You trying to get me drunk?"

"Maybe," Horace said, smiling. "You look like you've had a rough day."

"We've all had a rough fucking day. It's not like everyone's flush with a Mercy commission. Aren't you worried about the deaths?"

"Not really," Horace said. "I know it's only men that are dying, but most of them died pretty much right around the same time. Since I haven't bought it yet, I figure that I'm okay." They clinked glasses and drank. This time Mrs. Miller filled the glasses.

"Well?" she said, holding up the shot glass.

"I need to let mine sit a little bit," Horace said. Mrs. Miller shrugged and drank. "So, what are *you* doing here so early?"

"I'm fucking hiding."

"Best place for it."

"Look," Mrs. Miller said, scraping a thumbnail over the whiskey bottle's label, "it's a small town, and everyone knows my husband isn't worth a shit. He's been leaving me and the kids for longer and longer periods. He doesn't help me with anything at home. It just sucks. I have a good job and don't need him to help with the bills or anything. It's just that since he's been gone, physically and emotionally, it's been hard on me. I have to do all the parenting myself and take care of the house myself. Sometimes I just want to get away and forget my life for a bit."

"Your kids aren't little anymore," Horace said.

"That helps because they can pretty much take care of themselves, but I feel like I don't know them anymore. They don't really talk to me about anything."

"My kids are like that too," Horace said. "They have no use for me unless they want something. I just got all this money, and I'm going to spend it on them or the wife. What about what I want? I earned the money. I should be able to be a bit frivolous with it." Mrs. Miller flicked his shot glass with her finger. He picked it up and drank.

"How's your wife?"

"Not too great," he said. "I think she's cheating on me. I don't have any proof. It's just a feeling I have."

"Maybe we should have gotten married to each other instead. Get your shit cut so there'd be no chance of having kids. Then we could spend every fucking night in this shithole drinking." She laughed, and Mr. Green joined her.

"That would be a perfect life," he said. Mrs. Miller felt his hand touch her knee under the table. She pulled back.

"Keep your hands to yourself," she said. "We're just having a conversation."

"Well, why not?" He poured another shot and drank it, putting the bottle down and not filling her glass. "Your husband is a loser, and my wife is worthless. Let's cut loose just for tonight. Let's get drunk and fuck."

"Nope," Mrs. Miller said. "Not interested."

"Bombed out, huh? No go. Shit." Horace Green stood up. "Speaking of bombs. I'm thinking of starting a company that makes land mines shaped like prayer mats. Prophets will go through the roof!" Horace Green's head exploded, covering Mrs. Miller with gore. She picked his ear out of her shot glass and tossed it on the floor.

"Interesting," Mrs. Miller said. She got out of the booth and went over to the bar. The bartender had ducked for cover and was beginning to get up but he froze, hunched over, and clutched his stomach.

"I think I pissed myself," he said. Mrs. Miller reached over the bar and tapped him on the back.

"Tell me a joke," she said.

"What?"

"Just tell me a fucking joke." Mrs. Miller slapped him on the back.

"Fine, just don't fucking touch me. Oh, god, I think I actually pissed myself." Mrs. Miller took a bottle of Booths Vodka from the rail. She poured a drink and handed it down to the bartender, who took a sip and waved a hand in thanks.

"I tried to catch fog today," the bartender said. "I mist." He stayed in that hunched position. Mrs. Miller took a drink from the bottle and waited. Nothing. She spied a man at the end of the bar. He had his head in his hands and was crying. She walked over to him and sat down.

"We're all going to die," he said.

Mrs. Miller looked at his wizened face and shabby clothing. She had no idea who he was.

"Tell me a joke," she said.

"Life is a joke," he replied.

"Tell me a joke, and I'll give you this vodka," she said. He wiped his tears and registered the bottle.

"What did the fish say when it hit a wall?" the man said. "Dam." His head exploded. His body slumped to the floor.

"A deal's a deal," Mrs. Miller said, putting the vodka bottle next to his body. She stepped over him, careful not to slip on the blood on the floor, and left the bar.

Chapter 8

Joyce & Chip Miller

"Here's the contact number if you have any further questions or concerns." The military man handed Joyce a card. Behind him, two soldiers were wheeling out the body of Marky. He was in a body bag, and the stretcher was clean, but Joyce couldn't help thinking about her upstairs bedroom. Thinking about all the blood and bits that were everywhere she looked. Thinking about how nobody offered to help her clean it up.

"What do I do about the upstairs?" Joyce said. "What do I do about all the blood and stuff?"

"We don't do any of that," the military man said. "We just handle the scene." He tapped the card in her hand. "Call them. They'll be able to help you get in touch with a bioremediation crew that can clean up. There are a couple places they can recommend that can help with this. I wouldn't recommend trying to clean it up yourself."

"How quickly can they get here?" Joyce said.

"Not quickly," the military man said. "Usually, these types of cleanings are handled discreet and compassionately. But I've got to tell you; they're backed up with so many deaths. We can't send out for our of town crews because we don't really know what's happening here yet. We have to maintain the quarantine. Some National Guard soldiers are in training for this as we speak. I know that doesn't help you now. I would suggest calling that number and getting on the list for cleaning. In the meantime, close the door to your room and stay out of there."

"Alright," Joyce said. She put the card on an end table. There was a loud thump from upstairs. The military man looked up toward the sound.

"Did your brother see it happen?" he asked.

"No," Joyce said. "He was in his room."

"Better not let him see it. He'll probably be curious, but keep him away. The things you see with your eyes are forever in your brain. Might give him nightmares."

"You don't know my brother," Joyce said. The military man put his helmet back on.

"I've got to go," he said. "Call that number."

"I will," Joyce said. She followed behind the military man and closed the door behind him as he left. Something upstairs began screaming. The sound was high-pitched and wailing. Not like her brother's low mumble at all. Joyce ran up the stairs. Her brow furrowed. She clenched her teeth so hard they ground audibly. She smacked the door with the palm of her hand.

"Open up, Chip!" she said. The screaming stopped. Chip opened the door. His dark hair was splayed over his forehead. He smelled like sour milk.

"What?" he said.

"You tell me," Joyce said. "I know you have something to do with this. Whatever weird stuff you have going on in here needs to stop."

"You know I've been summoning demons since the fourth grade," Chip said.

"This is different," Joyce said. "Something is off. The banging around and the screaming isn't like it used to be."

"I'm trying new stuff. It's not like I can control it." Chip stepped forward out of the way of a pocket knife as it zipped past him and stuck into the door frame.

"You're on fire, Chip," Joyce said, gesturing at Chip's pants leg. Chip looked down and slapped the small fire off his jeans.

"Okay," Chip said. "I've been having some problems."

"Do you know what's going on around here?"

"Come in," Chip said, stepping away from the door. Joyce walked into the room, stepping into a circle of salt Chip made for visitors. The screaming began again just as she entered the circle. Joyce covered her ears.

"Can't you say some ancient incantation to make this stop?" Joyce yelled.

"Sure," Chip said. He raised his hands to the ceiling. "SHUT THE FUCK UP!" The screaming stopped. Inanimate objects that were flying around the room fell to the floor. The lights turned on.

"That works?" Joyce said.

"They speak English," Chip said.

"Chip, tell me what's going on. I want to help you." Joyce sat down in the middle of the circle. There was no way she trusted leaving, even with things seeming okay for the moment. Chip sat down outside of the circle across from her. He clasped his hands together, rubbing them. She'd never seen him look so nervous before.

"I think this is my fault," he said. "I was trying to kill Dad."

"Why would you want to kill Dad?"

"You know why," Chip said. His eyes went black. "He's always leaving us, and there will be a time when he doesn't come back. It's messing with Mom. She's pissed off at him, but now it seems like she's getting pissed off at us because of him. I know that doesn't make sense when I say it out loud, but it's the feeling I have. It's like she's beginning to hate us. Every time that

Dad leaves, I think he's finally going to stay gone, and we can move on with things, but he keeps coming back. I'm sick of it. I wanted him to stay gone so that we can save our relationship with Mom." The lights began flickering, and even when they came back on completely, shadows lingered.

"I don't think what Dad is doing has anything to do with Mom." Joyce checked the salt circle to make sure there weren't any gaps.

"Don't you think Mom is acting weird?" Chip said.

"Mom has to work and take care of us. She pays for everything here. That's a lot of stress."

"But it isn't our fault," Chip said. "We didn't ask to be born. We didn't make this stress. What are we supposed to do? Not exist? Bullshit."

"So killing dad makes this all better?" Joyce stood up. "Dad is a fucking asshole, but it's been a long time since I've wanted or expected anything from him."

"It's not just about Mom," Chip said. "It's about me. Dad isn't around. He wasn't there when I learned how to tie a tie. He wasn't there to show me how to shave."

"That's all shit you can learn on YouTube."

"I don't want to learn it on fucking YouTube!"

"Fine then!" Joyce kicked the salt from her circle. The screams were coming again. The ground began to tremble. Joyce didn't care. She just wanted all of this to stop. "Kill dad! I don't give a fuck, but stop this thing from killing everyone else. are good dads out there who are dying and don't deserve it. Stop it, Chip."

"I don't know how," Chip said, his eyes downcast. For a moment, he looked very young to Joyce. Her little brother came back to her. The brother before he got all weird with his occult stuff and only-black wardrobe. She almost hugged him, but remembered that she didn't really like him then either. Chip looked back up at her and kept talking.

"I tried to curse dad, but he must be gone. He was the only one meant to die, but if he's gone, others will be targeted, and there's nothing I can do to stop it."

"So if dad is gone for good?"

"If dad is gone for good, then every other dad in this town is fucked." Joyce felt the air in the room chill. She went to the door.

"You've got to fix this, Chip," she said.

"I'll figure it out." Joyce opened the door but paused before leaving.

"Marky's guts are all over my room. Don't go in there." She closed the door behind her.

Chapter 9

Mr. Miller & Heidi the Stripper

The gravel parking lot felt like it was teetering to Mr. Miller as he tried making his way back to his motel room. Heidi was tugging at his arm. She gave him a quick kick in the ass, which put a little pep in his step.

"Holy crap, you drank too much," Heidi said. "Keep walking. There's no way in hell that I'm going to be able to carry you."

"Thank you so much for taking me home," Mr. Miller said. He took an off-step which almost made him tumble. "I should have stopped at six beers."

"You should have stopped at three," Heidi said, pulling him by the belt. She got to the door and plunged a hand into his pocket.

"Easy does it there," Mr. Miller said. "You might touch my dick."

"I doubt you could get a hard-on if you tried. I'm just going for the room key. Once I get you plonked down on your bed, I'm going back to work. Who knows how much money I've lost in messing with you."

"There's nobody fucking in there. It's been dead all night," Mr. Miller said. Heidi got the keys and ripped them out of his pocket. She unlocked the door and hauled him inside. The room's funky smell made his nostrils wrinkle. She pulled him to the bed and dropped him.

"I'm leaving the keys right here," she said.

"Wait. Wait!" Mr. Miller said. "Stay with me for a bit. I have some booze in the suitcase. There's some plastic cups by the ice bucket."

"You got ice?"

Mr. Miller shook his head. "Broken." Heidi opened the suitcase and found a fifth of tequila. She took the bottle over to the cups and poured two glasses. Mr. Miller sat up on the bed and held out his hand for a cup.

"Thanks," he said. Heidi took a drink and put her cup down on the table.

"What the hell are you doing here anyway?"

"Wife...kids..."

"You going to them or going away from them?"

"It's not easy," Mr. Miller said, holding out his cup. She filled it, pouring the rest of the bottle into it. She shook her head.

"Just another man leaving his family. You're nothing new. Same shit happens every day."

"It's not easy. I've tried, but it's just not for me. Every day the same thing. Same shit."

"The shit is that you can run and leave them, and your wife will have to pick up the pieces herself. What's she going to do? Can she run off and leave the family? It's shit that the man is the only one who seems to have that option. Where are you going to go anyway?"

"West. I have a brother in Colorado. I can work for him. Hydroponics."

"And you're going to send money home?"

"That bitch is going to take me for everything I've got. She has a good job. She doesn't need my money."

"She might not," Heidi said, "but your kids will."

"What the fuck do you know about it anyway?" Mr. Miller's voice was becoming a whisper. He took a drink, liquor spilling down the corners of his mouth. "You're just some stripper in the middle of nowhere. You've got to be running from something too."

"We're all running from something," Heidi said. Walking to the foot of the bed, she lifted her shirt over her head. Mr. Miller watched her through half-closed eyes. She stroked her hand down the center of her body and gripped her right love handle. Pulling her hand around her stomach, she unzipped a gaping flesh maw. The skin sagged around the edges, showing sallow glimpses of herbivore teeth in pinkish gums. She took both hands and pulled the upper lip open, revealing a tongue dabbled in inch-long flesh spikes. Mr. Miller looked inside Heidi the stripper. He looked down the gullet of the mouth, beyond the grayish-white of her lower ribcage, where a black pit extended lower than her intestines. He tried to get up, but it was a feeble attempt, and he sank back down upon the bed. His tequila spilled out of his fallen cup. Heidi picked up one of his legs and moved her stomach over it. It closed down upon it and sucked, pulling him in up to the knee.

"Oh, my god, you feel so good," Heidi said. "You're going to be with me for a while."

Mr. Miller began to scream. Heidi stepped backward, pulling him off the bed by her stomach maw. He hit his head on the carpeting with a loud thump. He groaned. She took the tequila bottle off the table and smashed him on the side of the temple. Mr. Miller stopped groaning. His eyes, now wide open, looked up at the stained ceiling. Heidi's stomach sucked, and he went inside up to his crotch. His freed leg pushed tightly against her.

There was a knock at the door.

"Hey!" The motel clerk screamed from outside. "I knew you were going to try some shit! Let me in! It's thirty-five for one person. I know you got two in there!" He continued to hammer at the door. Heidi reached into Mr. Miller's pockets and came out with his car keys.

"Not my Honda," Mr. Miller wheezed. Heidi's stomach mouth sucked, but couldn't take any more of Mr. Miller inside because of the leg.

"Get it together," Heidi said, slapping the side of her stomach.

The motel clerk kept yelling. "You owe me money! You're not sleeping until I get paid! This isn't a free for all here. This is a place of business!"

Heidi's stomach sucked harder, and Mr. Miller's free leg bent backward, lying with his knee to his chest, his foot in his face. Mr. Miller kept talking about his Honda. Heidi put her hands on his shoulder and pulled the rest of him into her. When his head was behind her stomach teeth, she reached to her left and drew her hand across her stomach, closing the mouth. She put her shirt back on, opened the motel door, and looked at the angry ferret motel clerk outside.

"You can't stay here unless he pays!"

"I'm not staying," Heidi said. "I'm working."

"You're whoring it up in my motel."

"I'm dropping off a drunk client. He's in the bathroom taking a cold shower. You can see his luggage. I'm going back to work." The clerk looked around her and took a step back.

"I'm going to be watching," he said.

"If you really want to see something," Heidi said, "then come on over after your shift and see me at the Stallion."

The motel clerk blushed,is weeping acne flushing a Crayola red. Heidi touched his cheek and gave a little laugh. He slapped her hand away, said something about whores, and returned to his office. Heidi took Mr. Miller's car keys and unlocked the Honda. She drove out of the parking lot, down the highway, and into the night.

Chapter 10

MARFT

Mrs. Miller wasn't sure what she would find at her husband's Elk's Lodge, but this was a disappointment. The 'Great Hall' was a large room with rectangular folding tables set up end to end along the whole middle length. The cheap linoleum flooring was chipped and dirty. The white-painted wood paneling walls held the sickly yellowing from years of cigarette smoke. Metal folding chairs of different types and relative safety were neatly pushed into the table. There was a podium set up at the head of the hall. It was placed on a raised platform made of plywood and 2x4s. There was a flag on either side of the podium; American to the left and a green one with an Elk and the inscription #32475 on the right.

"Pathetic," she said, walking over and opening every window she could. The air was as stale as the furnishings. Mrs. Smith walked in behind her. She was a stout woman with clear skin and a face so beautiful it made several of the women in town severely jealous.

"Hello," Ms. Smith said. "So this is the place we're not allowed to be?"

"Secret lodge bullshit," Mrs. Miller said, trailing a finger through the dust on a window ledge. "With how much my husband talked about it, I thought it would be cleaner. Leather chairs and a big cigar humidor."

"I saw a fireplace with a roaring fire and a bar full of expensive single malts. I saw a long table that didn't have legs you could fold up." They laughed together. It felt good to Mrs. Miller.

She remembered being much better friends with Ms. Smith than they were now. They used to sit on the porch having drinks and talking the night away. They met at the library book club and always recommended books that were made into a movie. They spent the book club meetings eating snacks and mingling. When it came time to talk about the book, it was time to rent the movie and watch it together at either of their homes. Ms. Smith was the first smiling face she looked for in a crowd. Not anymore.

Mrs. Miller thought about a night when she wondered if their relationship was really a friendship, or something that skipped along the surface. She never really remembered sharing any secrets with Ms. Smith. No speaking about her future hopes and dreams. No trying to commiserate over problems at home. She couldn't remember anything. So one night after they watched 'I Robot' to prep for that Saturday's book club, she tried something.

Ms. Smith was beautiful, everyone saw that, but she didn't see it herself on account of her weight. When Ms. Smith made an offhand comment about how thin she looked, Mrs. Miller went for it. She remembered telling Ms. Smith about how her biological parents starved her as a child. That social services were called after her pediatrician suspected neglect. That she lived in foster homes until she aged out without a family. Nobody wanted to adopt her, and she never really understood why. And her thinness? That was because of the starving. There was something about a failure to thrive diagnosis from the doctors. The truth was that no matter how much she ate, she would never be able to pack on the pounds. Her body didn't work that way. It wasn't an exercise program or a diet. It was just her. She was a living monument to abuse. After she spilled the beans to Ms. Smith, Mrs. Miller recalled her face. She wouldn't look at her, and she sputtered around as if trying to figure out something to say. Finally, it happened.

"Well, I have such trouble myself," Ms. Smith said. "Maybe my parents should have starved me too! Maybe I could have a figure like yours!"

That was it for Mrs. Miller. After that, she stopped calling on Ms. Smith, and their friendship fizzled to nothing.

"What do you think they did here?" Ms. Smith said.

"Hired strippers. Snorted blow. Bet on horses. Gave each other hand jobs and high-fives all night. I don't know." Mrs. Miller went up to the podium and looked behind it. There was a notepad on a small shelf behind the podium base. The marking said 'Meeting Minutes' at the top. There was a quick scrawl about gathering food for a Thanksgiving food drive and a date back in 2014. The rest of the pages were blank.

"I doubt my husband wanted anything to do with strippers," Ms. Smith said. "The only time he could get it up was when the Utah Jazz won by at least ten points. I never knew if he was fucking me or picturing Jordan Clarkson." She stopped talking for a moment and then looked at the floor. "I don't know if I'm ever going to be able to clean his blood off the floor. It seeped into the wood..."

"I swear there must be a secret room or trap door or something," Mrs. Miller said, cutting Ms. Smith off. "This place sucks."

"It will have to do. The ladies will be here soon and we have to get this sorted."

"Do you really think they'll go for it?" Mrs. Miller said.

"This is not just something we want, but something we deserve," Ms. Smith said. "I'm tired of playing second fiddle to men. It's time we had our just due."

There was a rapping at the open great hall door, and women began walking into the room. Ms. Fisher led the way, being the one who always seemed to need to be first. Ms. Adams held Ms. Booth by the elbow. Mrs. Miller knew that Ms. Booth's husband was one of the first to die. Mr. Booth owned the Eggselent Diner on Main Street and was well known for joshing with his customers over their omelets and toast- all of it burnt more often than not. Mrs. Miller constantly asked him to buy a new toaster for the diner, but he refused, saying he would have to raise his prices.

"If I could afford a new toaster," Mr. Booth said, "I would buy one. CRUST me!" He would laugh at himself, and many of the other men in the diner would join in. She'd heard the same joke from him many times, but it always seemed to amuse him. Ms. Booth was taking his death pretty hard. Mrs. Miller thought she would have to make sure she gave her condolences. She stopped for a moment and wondered if she had ever heard Ms. Booth's voice before, since Mr. Booth did so much talking, she'd never really remembered actually hearing her speak. Ms. Evans and Ms. White came in next, followed by Ms. Young, who was so aged and wizened that it almost hurt to say her name.

"Welcome," Ms. Smith said. "Please take a seat at the table, and we can get down to business."

"What is this all about?" Ms. Fisher said. She took a seat near the podium and grimaced at her surroundings. The ladies all sat down, their faces frowning at the metal folding chairs. Ms. Kelly came in late, making her apologies. She had long red hair which frizzed out from her head in a triangle. She sat down by Ms. Adams, and they greeted each other amiably. Ms. Adams was a hairdresser and had cut Ms. Kelly's hair since the 90s. Everyone hated the haircut, even Ms. Kelly, but she kept going because she didn't want to hurt their friendship. Everyone also knew that Ms. Adams knew that Ms. Kelly hated the haircut, but she kept doing it out of spite because Ms. Kelly's nephew got her daughter pregnant, and they had to go out of state to get an abortion. An event whispered so much in town that Ms. Kelly stopped attending church due to the marked intensity of the stares of the other parishioners.

"This is about equality. This is about recognition. This is about dad jokes." Ms. Smith said 'dad jokes' in a tone biting with sarcasm. "The fact that we as women aren't recognized for our humor must come to an end. Are men the only type of creature on earth that comes up with puns? Shouldn't we be allowed the same regard as to the depth of our humor?"

"Really?" Ms. White said. "This is why we're here?"

"It may seem trite at first," Ms. Smith said. "I understand. But this isn't just about this situation and circumstance. This is just one area where we have been relegated to second-class citizens. Yes, there have been advances in equality over the years, but acknowledging history doesn't preclude anyone from seeing the current inequalities that exist and have been perpetually and systematically oppressing us and the rest of womankind."

"HOGWASH!" the ladies turned toward the door. Mr. Lance stood there with his hands out in front of him, thumbs hooked through suspenders stretched to breaking over his copious belly.

"What are you doing here?" Mrs. Miller said. "This is a closed meeting."

"It's trash day. Every Thursday, I come out here to ensure the bins are set out for Friday morning pickup. What are you doing here? This isn't your club."

"We chose to meet here to discuss the plans for our new movement. Since so many men are dead, we felt that you wouldn't be needing it."

"Well, I don't see anything wrong with that," Mr. Lance said. "What are you doing?"

"It's private."

"I was listening for a bit outside in the hallway," Mr. Lance said, pointing obviously to the doorway. "I think I belong in this meeting." Mr. Lance stood where he was, looking at the floor, actually scuffing the floor with his right foot.

"Fine," Mrs. Miller said. "Sit down, but don't say anything." Mr. Lance sat down on a chair at the end of the table. He nodded politely at the other ladies, who smiled at him in turn. Mr. Lance was known to help with odd jobs in the community. He was primarily known to handle those odd jobs at married women's homes while their husbands were working.

"As I was saying," Ms. Smith said. "The deaths involving dad jokes are sexist, classist, racist, and all other sorts of 'ists. Pick an 'ist, and it's 'ists."

"I don't get it," Ms. Adams said. "Why would we want to be a part of the whole dad joke thing? They're dying. I don't want my head to explode." The other ladies nodded in agreement. Mr. Lance sat passively in his seat.

"It's not the dying that's the problem. It's the cause of death. We are being oppressed and suppressed by the town curse! It's the curse that must be canceled, both figuratively and literally. Save our dads, yes! But also save equality in our society."

Mr. Lance began pounding on the table and cheering, realized that nobody else was doing it, and sheepishly stopped.

"So, I was thinking," Ms. Smith continued, "of starting an advocacy group called Moms Are Really Funny Too! A panel of mothers who want the world to acknowledge our humor as valid and amusing to the same degree as dad jokes."

"MARFT?" Mr. Lance said. "That's your group?"

"We can work on the acronym," Ms. Smith said. "It can be the first discussion in the panel."

"What about me?" Mr. Lance said.

"I don't know. What about you?"

"Why can't I join MARFT?" Mr. Lance held his hands out in a supplicating gesture. Ms. Fisher held his hand and squeezed it.

"You can't join MARFT, acronym pending. You're a man."

"But I'm discriminated against too!" Mr. Lance said, getting to his feet. Tears began welling in his eyes. Ms. Fisher wouldn't let go of his hand.

"You're a man," Ms. Smith said.

"Yes," Mr. Lance said. "I am a man. I am a red-blooded-America-loving man! But I am not a dad. Watch this. Mr. Lance took a crumpled piece of paper out of his pocket, smoothed it out on his pants leg, and read. "Why didn't the crab share his lunch? Because he was shellfish!" He put the paper down and raised his hands in the air. Seconds passed. The women watched his ponderous belly undulate with his breathing.

"Is that all?" Ms. Smith said.

"Can't you see? Can't you see?" Mr. Lance waved his hands around. "Can't you see that I'm impervious to the curse? I don't explode! I've been walking around telling these shitty jokes for days, and nothing happens. NOTHING! You see, I've been feeling a little down lately, and I just decided I wanted to die." Three of the women gasped. The rest of them did too, but silently. "I wanted to explode and be no more. I've been so lonely since my wife died from cancer three years ago. So very lonely. I didn't want to live anymore, but then I found that I couldn't die, and then I figured out why...I'm not a dad!"

Nobody gasped this time. It was palpably silent. Mr. Lance felt like his big reveal was a dud.

"So, you want to join MARFT?" Ms. Smith said.

"I am MARFT," Mr. Lance said. "I can tell dad jokes until I'm blue in the face, but I won't die. My head doesn't explode and send bits of myself everywhere. It was then that I hit rock bottom. It's been coming for years now. When my wife was dying from cancer, I couldn't keep up with the messages and visits from my friends, family, and community. After she died, it was like I lost my friends too. They stopped inviting me to places. They stopped coming by. Soon, I was all alone. The phone just stopped ringing. I mean, it was crazy how fast it happened. In like a year, I was alone."

Ms. Booth put her hand on his stomach and gave it a reassuring squeeze. She started rubbing his gut in a clockwise motion. Mr. Lance ignored her. "Alone," he continued. "When I tried to kill myself in the way that other men are dying and I couldn't do it, it was like I was even cut off from my own gender identity. I may not be a dad, but I am a man. A MAN! I deserve equal rights. You say you are MARFT? I am MARFT!"

"Fine, you're MARFT," Mrs. Miller said. "Sit down and shut the fuck up for a minute."

Mr. Lance sat down and shut the fuck up.

"Alright," Mrs. Miller continued. "We moms are done being denied our God-given right for equal hilarity with dads. Just last week, I was cleaning out the gutters, because I can't ever get Mr. Miller to do anything, and the ladder I used to get on the roof fell over, so I was stuck! I had to wait for a neighbor to come by and wave him down to help me. It was like a French comedy of errors!" There was laughter coming from every mom in the audience. All except for Mr. Lance, who was sitting with his hands crossed in front of him.

"That's not funny," Mr. Lance said. "Why is everyone laughing?"

"It's a situational riot," Mrs. Miller said. "Just like Ms. White last week at the grocery store. She had that faulty cart that dogged right. She bumped into an endcap and knocked down some detergent sample pods." The women began laughing louder. Mr. Lance stood up.

"That isn't funny!" he said. "Telling a story where you acted like an idiot or did something a little off isn't a dad joke. You're only hitting slightly amusing."

"It's not up to you, a man, to tell us what is funny. We know what is funny."

"I don't think you do," Mr. Lance said.

"Well then, by all means, show us, Mr. Lance. Since you know all about dad jokes."

Mr. Lance walked up to the podium. Mrs. Miller was very extra in the way she bowed him up to the platform. Mr. Lance cleared his throat and began.

"What time do you go to the dentist? Tooth hurty. How could I tell the frog was in a good mood? He was hoppy." The women glared at him. None of them were laughing. Mr. Lance began to sweat. "Why did the football player go to the bank? To get his quarterback. Why couldn't the leopard hide? He was spotted." Mrs. Miller pushed Mr. Lance away from the podium. He went meekly aside.

"THAT isn't funny," Mrs. Miller said. "I think we all agree on that."

"Dad jokes are just simple puns," Mr. Lance said. "They're just stupid and fun."

"That's the problem," Mrs. Miller said, pounding her fist on the podium, shaking it to its press-board foundations. "That is the inequality."

"It is what it is," Mr. Lance said.

"Maybe so, but that is all in the past. It's time for a new age of comedic discourse between women and men. What did Malcolm X say?" The moms stood up and shouted in chorus.

"BY ANY MEANS NECESSARY!"

"You're goddamn right!" Mrs. Miller said. "Let's take to the fucking streets!" The women grabbed at their weapons. Pistols were brought forth from handbags. Stilettos were drawn from hidden pockets. Ms. Booth took a grenade out of her bra.

"What the fuck, Ms. Booth?" Mr. Lance said.

"Are you MARFT or not?" she said.

"I am MARFT." Mr. Lance took a Swiss-Army knife out of his pocket and unfolded the corkscrew. "The knife is broken," he said.

"Let's take to the streets!" Mrs. Miller said. They poured out from the Elks Lodge, screaming like a pack of hounds from hell. Two members of the National Guard looked up and reached for their sidearms.

Chapter 11

Heidi the Stripper and Mr. Miller

Heidi got into the Honda, pushing the seat as far back as it would go. She leaned back and to the side, finding that she could reach the pedals. Steering would be tough. Mr. Miller was swelling her stomach. She tapped the GPS, looking at the address history. Frowning, she slapped her stomach.

"What's your address?" she said. She heard a muffled voice from inside her. She reached down, opening up a small hole in her stomach.

"Hand me your driver's license," she said, sticking her hand into her stomach. White frothy goo, much like spittle, started bubbling around her wrist. There was some jostling from inside her, but after a few moments, she withdrew her hand with a sticky license in her grip.

"Is this current?" she asked. There was a muffled sound from within her. She nodded and punched the address into the GPS. She rolled out of the motel parking lot and took off down the highway.

After an hour, she pulled into Miller's driveway. She got ponderously out of the Honda, giving it a withering look as she walked up the porch steps and knocked. She waited, cradling her belly with both hands. Chip answered the door.

"I have someone that belongs to you," she said.

"Who are you?" Chip asked.

"Come on, kid," Heidi said, pushing him aside and waddling into the living room. "You look like a weird kid who's into weird stuff, so I won't beat around the bush. I have someone in my stomach that belongs to you."

"In your stomach?"

"That's what I said. Now help me sit down on the couch and give me a hand with him."

"Who is it?"

"I'll give you three guesses." Chip took her by the arm and helped her over to the couch. She sat down, leaning back and allowing her stomach to bulge. She lifted her shirt to expose her belly. Chip looked at the flesh being pressed from the inside by groping fingers.

"Look away if you're squeamish," Heidi said, "but you'll have to help pull. He's been cooped up in there for a while, and they cramp up after a bit." Chip nodded, keeping his eyes on her stomach. Heidi reached down to her side and pulled her hand across, opening her stomach maw. Two hands reached out, waving in the air. Chip took them and began to pull. Heidi let her head fall back. She moaned as Chip pulled.

"Pull harder!" Heidi said. Chip lay back, digging his heels into the carpet. Heidi covered her mouth with her hands, stifling a scream as Mr. Miller came out of her.

"Holy shit!" Chip said, then dropped the hands.

"Pull him out!" Heidi screamed. Chip pulled. His father slurped out of her belly and lay in the fetal position on the floor. He was breathing hard, his body shuddering. Heidi closed up her stomach and stood up. She stretched her back and pulled her clothing back into place.

"He'll be alright," Heidi said.

"Who are you?" Chip said.

"I'm Heidi. I bring them back." She walked out the front door and closed it behind her. Chip watched her walk away down the block and then turned back to his father. He was trying to wipe the muck from his face and not doing too well. Chip got him a towel from the bathroom and dropped it into his hands.

"Welcome back, dad."

Chapter 12

Joyce Miller, Officer McFiggis, and Officer McFiggis's Shotgun

The bum was sleeping next to an industrial trash bin in an alley between the Slapshot Bar and Auntie May's Cookies. She was lying mostly inside a sleeping bag nestled within a refrigerator box. Her head was outside the box, her hair spreading out around her head and becoming damp and filthy from alley debris. A thin ray of light permeated the alley and ran along the breadth of it, dead center. The light fell over her forehead, but a new shadow blocked it. Officer McFiggis stood above her, looking down and frowning. The shotgun dropped down in his right hand, but the barrel seemed to jerk and jump to point at the bum.

The shotgun knew this would have to be quick. The alley wasn't very large, but Officer McFiggis was. Anyone passing by would see them. He was almost jumping out of his zinc to put his shell in her. He thought about all the wasted years of shelling targets or blowing his load out into nothing. This was the real stuff right here. Officer McFiggis made him a man, and there was no turning back now. He wondered why McFiggis wasn't listening to him.

She's the one. Do it. I'm ready to explode!

"She's just a bum," McFiggis said. "Let's just leave her alone."

Sweety-honey-baby-love, that's not the way. You've got me all riled up here. You can't just leave me all hot and bothered like this. Are you just a tease?

"It's not like that," McFiggis said. "Let me just take you home and give you a good oiling.

I'm not some young gun. I'm not easily appeased anymore. Let's do it.

The woman opened her eyes for a moment. She blinked up at Officer McFiggis and then rolled onto her side and began to snore. Officer McFiggis wrinkled his nose at the strong smell of piss that emanated from her. The shotgun twitched in his hand. He looked down the alley. He heard fresh screaming. There were gunshots and orders being shouted over bullhorns. More gunshots and more screams, and then the sound of a car crash. What new hell was going on now? The shotgun barrel slapped him on the skin.

Let me into this woman, and then we can see what's going on. Bust me out on her, and we'll go, but do this first.

"I know her," McFiggis said. "She used to cashier at the supermarket and do a radio show late night on weekends. She's not bad. It's just that the drugs have her now."

Is this because I'm one percent manganese? Is that why you won't let me have her? Are you racist?

"Fuck no," Officer McFiggis said. "If I were racist, I would go after your chromium."

I am a beautiful alloy. I thought you loved me.

"I don't love you. You can't love a gun. Not really. I have lots of guns in all shapes and sizes. You're no more special than the rest of them."

Now you're just trying to hurt me. After all we've been through together. It's not fair to me. I know you've had other guns. I've seen them around the house and in the safe. I've seen you slip them into your belt like it's nothing. I hate you so much for it, and that hate continues to boil inside of me, but I can't let you go. I love you, and I want to make this work.

"Killing people is wrong," Officer McFiggis said.

Nobody will know she's gone and it will be so good, baby. I will be so good you won't believe it. I know you want to feel it. I know you have to have it. Even if you won't do it for me, do it for yourself.

The shotgun raised, pointing into the side of the woman's face. She opened her eyes.

"I love you," Officer McFiggis said, squeezing the trigger and putting a hole the size of a can of Mountain Dew in the woman's head. Gore splattered. Officer McFiggis could see right through her face to the asphalt below. The shotgun quivered in his hand. He pumped another round in the chamber and shot the woman in the stomach. He pumped another round and blew off her right knee. Officer McFiggis felt like his eardrums had burst, but he kept pumping shells. It was so loud, but he knew it would be okay. The gunshots he heard were coming almost with a pause now. The screams were reverberating off the alley walls. He saw a woman run past the mouth of the alley. The two soldiers ran by. Sirens cut through the turmoil just as McFiggis thought he smelled smoke.

"It's hell out there," he said, pulling the trigger and separating her hand from her wrist. He pumped another round, but there was a jam. He cursed and sat down on the blood-soaked asphalt. The woman's eyes were still open and looking at him. How had that part of her face remained together? He couldn't say. He tried clearing the jam, but it wouldn't budge.

I'm so sorry. I'm getting old, and the gears don't work as well as they used to. Just give me a bit and I'll be ready to go again.

"MOM!" Joyce Miller stopped at the end of the alley and screamed. Officer McFiggis dug his fingers into the shotgun, pushing at the shell to make it move. Joyce heard him grunt and turned her head. Her mouth opened at the sight of the policeman covered in a juicy red shroud.

"Officer McFiggis? Are you okay?" Joyce said.

"What are you doing out here, Joyce," Officer McFiggis said.

"I'm looking for my mom."

"You should go home. Go home and hide." The shotgun twitched upwards. McFiggis pushed the barrel to the ground. "I've got a bad feeling that everything's about to go sideways. Go home, young woman." The shotgun began yammering.

Clear me out. She's a free one. Nobody knows she's here. Do her and leave her by the bum. It will be so good, and nobody will find out.

Officer McFiggis looked at Joyce. She didn't seem to hear what his gun was saying. He reached down and pumped hard at the shotgun. The jam wouldn't clear.

"I need to find my mother," Joyce said.

"Get out of here, Joyce. I've known your family for a long time. I'll find Mrs. Miller and get her home to you. Don't worry about it. Just go."

"Are you okay?" Joyce said, taking a step backward. Officer Mcfiggis slipped a bit in the gore. He wrenched at the shotgun, and a shell popped out from the side. He pumped the gun. A hard double-click, and it was loaded and ready again. He looked up at Joyce. A deep frown sprawled across the lower half of his face.

I'm ready to go.

Joyce turned to run. Officer McFiggis raised the shotgun and fired. The shot missed Joyce and hit the side of the bar. Before he loaded another round, Joyce was gone from the alley. But the marchers were there now. Women and men with their fists raised and shouting defiant rages. A soldier with a bloody face ran down the alley to escape them.

"Run!" he screamed. Officer McFiggis shot him in the chest. He chambered another round. The shotgun groaned.

I love you.

Chapter 13

MARFT, Officer McFiggis, and Officer McFiggis's Shotgun

Officer McFiggis gazed at the shotgun's smoking barrel. He wasn't going to run. He wasn't even sure that he could with his aching knees and a bad back. People told him that growing old was rough, but he didn't think it would be this bad in his early 50s. He pumped the shotgun. For a weapon he'd had for so long, it felt odd in his hands. It jerked around like it had a mind of its own. And that voice he was hearing, as if the shotgun was talking to him, made him more than a bit disconcerted. The police office had a therapist if he wanted to talk to somebody, but he didn't want to bring that sort of thing up. If he told the county shrink that his gun was talking to him, he figured he would get a mandatory vacation at the very least.

I know that you can hear me.

"I can hear you," Officer McFiggis said, thinking that maybe he actually *was* going crazy. He had about five years to go until retirement and wondered if he would make it.

I hear lots of people coming.

Officer McFiggis heard it too. The soldier he killed had told him to run, and he just gunned him down without really thinking about it. So he was a murderer now? There was something to flights of fancy, Officer McFiggis thought, that made you want to run with them. So far, he figured the murders could be hidden under all the craziness going on, but what about when things calmed down? Would he be able to stop killing? Did he want to? A big part of him felt exactly the same before all this happened, but the new part of him was nagging to shoot. Nagging to kill. Maybe he wasn't just listening to the voices in his head. Maybe he was under their control.

A truck crashed into the building at the end of the alley. A man got out and stumbled over to lie against the wall. A woman turned the corner and began stabbing him in the chest with a pair of sewing scissors.

"MARFT! MARFT! MARFT!" she was screaming over and over as she stabbed. Officer McFiggis walked calmly up to her and shot her between the shoulder blades. He loaded his gun as the stabbed man looked on, blood sliding from over fifteen stab wounds in his chest.

"What the hell is going on?" he said. Officer McFiggis blew his head off. He pumped the shotgun and rounded the corner. He saw a gang of women and a few men running through the streets. Some were starting fires. Some were attacking anyone they could get their hands on. He looked the opposite way down the street and saw the military setting up two blocks down. They created lines of soldiers flanking armored vans. Officer McFiggis walked into the middle of the road. A woman kicked through a car window and was grabbing at a screaming woman inside.

"Get your hands up," McFiggis said. She ignored him. He grabbed her by the hair and slammed her face into the car door. She fell into a gasping heap.

"Help me!" the woman in the car screamed. He reached into the broken window and opened the car door. He was grabbed from behind by two women. Their nails raked at his face. One pulled at his shotgun. He twisted his heavy frame, head-butting the face clawer and blasting the other's stomach through her spine.

Kill them! Kill them all!

The face clawer ripped his shirt and grabbed the .38 McFiggis had in a hidden holster. She pulled the trigger without pulling back the hammer and frowned at the gun before the shell made her chest explode. The woman in the car got out and ran away. McFiggis staggered and fell. Blood from the scratches clouded his vision. Canisters of tear gas bounced on the road around him. The military was making their move. MARFT rioters were surging forward. Tear gas canisters were picked up and thrown back at the soldiers. Rubber bullets strafed them, leaving them screaming and vomiting on the ground. Officer McFiggis got into the car and shut the door. His eyes began to burn from the gas, and he tried to close the car window before remembering it was broken. His glazing eyes watched the fighting all around him. He saw the dead and knew their names. He saw Ms. Smith on the ground, holding onto her ruined jaw. He saw Ms. Adams lying face down in a pool of blood. Fire was flowing over her clothing. He saw Mr. Lance being stomped by soldiers while he tried protecting his face. These were his people. This was his town. The town he was supposed to protect. The town he gave his life to. He saw Mrs. Miller, a bandana held over her mouth, escaping down an alley away from the fighting.

What do you have to say for yourself?

"Stop talking to me," McFiggis said.

Who was that?

"What?"

That gun the woman took off of you. Who was that?

"My .38," McFiggis said. The shotgun shifted, pointing the barrel at his head.

What do you have to say for yourself?

"I don't know what the fuck you're talking about," McFiggis said. A woman came up to the car. She was crying and talking, but he couldn't hear what she was saying. He gently pushed.

I've been loyal to you. I've always been there for you. I knew you were fucking around on me with other guns, but you'd always come back to me.

"I still don't understand."

For the last few days, it's felt like old times. It's like I was the only gun for you. You've taught me to fly.

A soldier came up to the car and pointed a rifle at him. McFiggis held up his badge, and he passed him on.

I thought I was okay with your philandering, but now I realize I'm not. I'm not just another piece. I'm not a part of your collection. I am worth your love and attention.

"You are special," Officer McFiggis said. His eyes burned. It was hard to breathe.

And you are special to me. I love you. But, honey?

"What?"

"*You've fucked around on me for the last time.*"

Officer McFiggis pulled the trigger. His head halved.

Chapter 14

Chip and Mr. Miller

Mr. Miller found the energy to stand up. His lower back hurt, but he felt it wasn't too bad an ache considering he had been engulfed by Heidi for so long. He wiped his hands down his sodden clothing, quickly realizing how vain the efforts were. He slicked his hair back and faced his son. He was taller than he remembered, even though he'd only seen him the other day. He'd realized he'd looked at his son, but hadn't *really* looked at him in a long time. He saw his son's solid jawline and the breadth of his shoulders. For a moment, he thought about how he used to hold him and tell him he loved him, that he would always be there for him. Then he caught Chip's look. Those dark eyes burrowing into him, judging him. Condemning him. It was not a look he relished but one he felt he deserved.

"Hello, Chip," Mr. Miller said.

"Dad," Chip said. Mr. Miller looked over his son into his dark and disheveled room. He saw the odd writings on the floor and his belongings piled against the walls.

"I know I haven't been there for you," Mr. Miller said. "But I want that all to change now."

"You've said that to me before," Chip said.

"I know, and I'm sorry. If I could change the past, I would, but I can't."

"When was it that you decided you didn't love us anymore? When did you decide that you didn't want to be my dad?" Mr. Miller shrugged and put on a grin that felt shitty to him.

"It wasn't a specific time," Mr. Miller said. "It's just kind of worn on me through the years. To be honest, I never really wanted to be a father, but when your sister came along, I thought it was the best thing to ever happen to me. The best thing. Some time went on, and I guess I began to feel angry. Angry at the time it took to raise a child. Angry at the cost."

"None of that is my fault," Chip said. The floor behind him began to smoke.

"I'm not blaming you," Mr. Miller said. "I'm just trying to be honest with you. For once. You're a young man, almost an adult. I think you can handle a little honesty."

"Well, I hope it's making you feel better," Chip said.

"I'm trying to apologize," Mr. Miller said. He was feeling desperate. "I'm trying to move forward."

"This is for you!" Chip said. "I'm not your therapist. I'm your son. You don't have to tell me you hated me and Joyce. We know. You think we want honesty? We don't need it. Your actions told us all we needed to know. It's not honesty we need. It's a father. Fathers don't lay all their shit on their children. They don't whine and bitch and moan about their problems. They're supposed to solve problems. They're supposed to be there for their kids. What's so wrong with me that you want to leave?"

"There's nothing wrong with you. It's my problem."

"Your problem has become all our problem," Chip said. "And you're not even man enough to have just cut ties and left a long time ago. You keep leaving and coming back and we're supposed just to be okay with it. Well, we're not okay, and it's your fault."

"You can't put all the blame on me," Mr. Miller said. "It's your mother too."

"At least she's here," Chip said. "At least she takes care of us, pays the bills, and helps us when we need it. Even if you have problems with her, don't let it hurt us."

"Well, I don't know what to do," Mr. Miller said. The smoke was condensing in the middle of the room. There were flashes of light coming from the center. The smoke blackened and spun in a tight vortex. "If you're not going to meet me halfway on any of this, I don't see why I should bother. I might have screwed up, but I deserve some mercy. I deserve some forgiveness. I want to try again. I want to start over. But it's going to take willingness on your part to try, or there's nothing left to say." Chip turned and walked into the bedroom. Mr. Miller followed. The door slammed shut behind them. He grabbed his son in a tight hug. Chip's body tensed, but Mr. Miller wouldn't let go.

"Let's try again," Mr. Miller said. "I can be a good father to you." Chip looked up at his dad. His eyes were brimming with tears. He gently pushed himself out of his father's embrace.

"This is all for you, Dad." Chip said, tears streaming down his face. Mr. Miller looked up, realizing that Chip wasn't the only thing looking at him. A creature hovered over Chip's head, its broad jaws open and slavering. The head wavered from side to side on a long sinewy neck. The red eyes locked on Mr. Miller's face.

"What in god's name is that?" Mr. Miller said.

"It's the end," Chip said. The creature's jaw flexed even wider, dropping low from a dislocating jaw. A hiss rose from deep inside. Chip grabbed his father and held him close. The creature lunged down, engulfing them both from their heads to their waists. It lifted them high. Their shoes scraped against the room's ceiling as they were turned upwards. Then the creature sank into the smoky vortex and vanished into the floor. The smoke dissipated from the room, leaving nothing to see. The door opened, letting light into the space.

Chapter 15

Joyce, Mrs. Miller, and Heidi the Stripper

Joyce was aware of the silence of the new morning. The living room shades were half-drawn, allowing the pinkish hue of the sunrise to chase shadows. She watched them crawl a bit before sitting up on the couch and shrugging down the comforter. Mrs. Miller was beginning to make noise in the kitchen.

"Do you want breakfast?" Mrs. Miller said.

"Did you make coffee?" Joyce said.

"I did."

"I'll just have that."

"Do you want an egg? I'm scrambling, and I think I made too much." Mrs. Miller poked her head into the room, her back arched so that Joyce could picture her holding an egg-laden skillet in a surplus of effort. *Just leave the damn thing on the stove.* Joyce hated feeling annoyed at her mother, especially since it was so often, and especially more since she knew something annoying was happening that she couldn't see. She knew it was going on and would sound like an idiot if she brought it up over a skillet.

"I don't want any eggs," Joyce said. "I'll just have coffee."

"Alright, dear." Her mother left, and Joyce heard the clang of a skillet as it was replaced on the stove.

"Mom?"

"What, dear?"

"When is my room going to be cleaned?" Joyce put her feet on the floor and pushed to her feet.

"Not for a bit. The cleaners are pretty backed up."

"I don't want to sleep on the couch anymore." Joyce took a coffee cup out of the cupboard. It read 'My Favorite Son-in-law gave me this cup' in black script on one side. A thrift store find. She poured herself a cup of black coffee and scalded her tongue on her first drink. Mrs. Miller scraped some eggs on her plate and the rest in the trash.

"If you want to clean up your boyfriend's brain matter, be my guest."

"He's not my boyfriend," Joyce said. She took another drink and kept scalding herself, thinking she never wanted to taste anything again.

"I have to go to work," Mrs. Miller said.

"Do you hear it?"

"Hear what?"

"Nothing." Joyce finished the cup of coffee, opened the front door, and stepped outside. Her mother followed right behind and looked out, her hands on her hips.

"They're gone," Mrs. Miller said. "Quarantine was over last night at ten. Didn't you hear them all leaving?"

"I guess I was tired. I went to bed before that. You could have woken me up."

"I thought I would let you sleep," Mrs. Miller said, placing a hand on Joyce's elbow. "I'll be back late tonight. I have a Zoom meeting with the board. I can't miss it."

"Mom, Chip is dead. Dad is dead."

"You don't know that."

"I can feel it," Joyce said. "They're gone."

"Well," Mrs. Miller put her arm around her daughter. "I know it's hard, but your father hasn't been present for a long time. You're too old to think that he would stick around."

"Not even for his kids," Joyce said. Her face was placid.

"Life has a way of telling you you're not enough. You weren't enough for your father to stay. I wasn't enough for your father to stay. Chip doesn't give a shit about anything."

"*Didn't* give a shit about anything. Past tense. He's dead. Doesn't that mean anything to you?"

"Of course it does," Mrs. Miller said.

"It doesn't look like it."

"We all process these things differently," Mrs. Miller said. "I've learned in my life, as you will too, that men just don't have what it takes. They don't stick around. They won't fight for us. But you know what? We don't need them. That's what's so funny about all of this. We don't need them at all."

"So, Chip?"

"Chip was just another man," Mrs. Miller said. "Not yet, just a kid, but well on his way." Joyce slunk her shoulder out of her mom's grasp.

"Have a good day at work, mom." Mrs. Miller got into her car and left.

Joyce went to the door and gazed inside her family home. She thought about the mess upstairs. She heard noises coming from upstairs and knew that even though her brother was dead, there were still dark things lurking there. She wondered how those things of shadows felt, knowing that her brother was gone. Maybe they were free to do what they wanted now that they were unfettered from their master. She felt that demons were probably much happier without masters. Joyce looked over to her left and saw her father's Honda in the driveway. He so loved that car, and she never understood why. She decided not to go into her house and instead went down the porch steps and to her father's car. The keys were in the ignition. She got inside the car and started it, immediately being hit with Dire Straits groaning about faggots becoming millionaires. She opened the glove box and found her father's old Tomtom GPS. She checked the address history and dialed in on the top address, hours away from where she was now. She hit seek on the radio and Whitney Houston shrilled about finding somebody. She backed out of the driveway and took off down the street.

Hours later, she was tooling down Hwy 61. Her mother called for the last couple of hours, but she never answered.

"Shut the fuck up," Joyce said, reaching down and turning off her volume settings. She was used to her mother bombarding her with calls, never really getting the hint that she hated the seemingly endless harassment. She smirked, thinking about how her mother wouldn't even realize she had left with her dad's car until later tonight, whenever she deigned to come home from work. She wondered what her mother would do, but nothing came to mind that bothered her. Joyce put her foot down on the gas, and the Honda's engine gave a pitiful roar.

"Predictable, reliable, and fucking boring," Joyce said. "Ever so bland." She tapped the GPS for no real reason. She was just three miles from the address, but had figured out where she was headed from about twenty miles before. The weathered road signs down this neglected strip of road were only about two things: Jesus and Strippers. The hand-painted signs flashed by every half mile. 'Find Jesus', 'Raging Stallion Gentlemen's Club', 'One Savior. One God', 'Girls, Girls, Girls', 'Pray and get Heaven', 'Pole Dancing and Buffet', 'Jesus Saves!', 'TOPLESS-JESUS-NUDE-SAVIOR-LEGS-HELL-SINNERS-FOOD-GOD-SEXY-LOVE...'

Joyce wondered why the hell her dad was going to a strip club. She didn't see her dad as the sort of guy who did that type of thing. And why this one? It didn't jibe with her. She remembered Chip was all bummed out a couple of years ago when he came back from sleeping over at a friend's house. He told her that his friend's dad had all these porn mags hidden behind his dresser. Chip spent the night paging through mag after mag of photos too glorious for words. His friend was well-used to the magazines and just wanted to play Risk, but Chip was having none of it.

"You have to give me one of these," Chip said.

"No way," his friend said. "My dad will know it's gone. Just get one from your own dad."

"My dad doesn't have any of these," Chip said. His friend squeak-roared a puberty-laden laugh.

"Every dad has porno mags," he said. "You just have to find them."

"Not my dad," Chip said, running his eyes over the feathered-haired sultry goddess.

"Yes, dipshit, even your dad." His friend took the magazine from under Chip's nose and put it back behind the dresser. Chip was so befuddled from what he'd just seen that he'd lost Risk in record time. He told Joyce that he went through his dad's things the first chance he got and found nothing stimulating. He carefully tossed the room, combing through every nook and cranny. Nothing.

"Our dad doesn't have any porn!" he wailed to Joyce.

"Pervert," Joyce said, slapping him lightly across the face before leaving.

A few years later, there was a news story about a famous porn star that died from an overdose. Her father shook his head after she showed him the article on her cell phone.

"That's why I don't get into that stuff," her dad said. "You never know if these girls are okay with what they're doing or if they're being coerced. It feels like human trafficking to me."

"Some people say that the sex industry is actually empowering women," Joyce said. Her father blinked at her for a moment, surprised at the statement. Then he shook his head.

"It just makes me feel uncomfortable," he said, and that was that.

Joyce pulled the Honda into the shared parking lot of the Raging Stallion Strip Club and a skeevy motel. The GPS showed that she had arrived.

"What the heck was my father doing here?" Joyce said aloud. She shut off the Honda and got out of the car. The motel clerk was sitting on a folding chair outside of the office. He called to her.

"You planning on staying?" he said.

"I don't know," Joyce said. "I think I'm going over there." She pointed to the strip club.

"Say no more," the clerk said. "I wish you well." He looked at her with his mouth open in a smile as if he might have more to say, but that was all. Joyce went over to the door of the strip club. The extra G on the sign was painted over with a black X. She stepped back as the bouncer shoved open the door. He stood, his eyes wide and staring off into the distance. He reached a hand into his pocket and took out a pack of cigarettes. He lit one with shaking hands, exhaling a long stream of smoke, and startling when he saw her.

"Sorry," Joyce said.

"You going inside?" he said.

"I'm looking for my father."

The man took another drag and shook his head. "Nobody in there is a father," he said. "Are you eighteen?"

"No."

"You should be eighteen before you go inside. Dancers have to be eighteen. Patrons twenty-one. That's the rules."

"Are you going to stop me if I try?" Joyce took a step toward the bouncer. He moved back, almost tripping over a lot refuse that might have once been alive. The bouncer swore under his breath and walked toward the other end of the building. Joyce went inside.

She saw swirling lights from a small twirling globe. She smelled old cigarettes and stale vomit. The lighting was too dark to notice dust or dirt, but the place emanated filth. Over at the bar, a semi-nude woman was feeding a thin, swarthy man into her stomach. Her head was lain back, her mouth open in quiet ecstasy. The stomach was puckering at the sides like it was sucking at the flailing man. All the kicking and fighting did nothing for him as he became a part of the woman's engorged belly. After he was inside her, she took her hand to her side and pulled along the edges of her stomach, closing up the hungry maw. She shook her head and tied her hair up in a ponytail, finally seeing Joyce at the door.

"Who are you?" Joyce said.

"I work here," she said. "I'm Heidi. Who are you?"

"I'm just looking for my father," Joyce said, eyeing the buffet table behind the woman. The food looked like it had been there for a while. The lunch meat seemed to shine out of the open plastic container.

"Your father was here," Heidi pointed to her stomach. Joyce walked toward her, her footsteps hesitant. She reached out a hand and touched Heidi's stomach on the closed-lipped scar line. Her hand was just barely under Heidi's drooping breasts. She felt a hand press against the inside of Heidi's stomach and press against hers. She pulled back.

"Your father was here," Heidi said. "He's not now."

The bouncer came back into the room. His glance stayed at the bar, now without a bartender, for a noticeable moment. Heidi pointed at the DJ booth next to the bar.

"Depeche Mode," she said. The bouncer went to the booth, reaching over the top and typing a few words on a laptop. Never Let Me Down began to play, but it came solid, a deeper bass line punctuating the already heavy low notes.

"Come with me," Heidi said, taking Joyce's hand and leading her to the dancing platform. Heidi rolled onto the stage and then helped Heidi up. The stripper began to sway with the music. Her body shifted with every note. A smile creased Joyce's face. She'd never seen someone so beautiful. Every wizened line of Heidi's face and every stretch mark on her hips formed a perfect sexual labyrinth. Joyce began to dance. The small disco bulb spun. The bouncer put out the lights, and their bodies were swathed in circular rainbows. Heidi reached over and slapped Joyce on the ass. The old stripper spun in a tight circle and fell off the stage, landing on her back and laughing up into the water-stained ceiling tiles. Joyce put her arms above her head. Her eyes closed. She twirled and laughed and forgave and felt freedom for the first time she could remember.

"No more," she said.

She jumped off the stage, landing next to Heidi. She grabbed her stomach and pulled. The maw fought against her, pursing its lips like a stubborn child. Joyce stabbed her fingers into it, feeling the wet warmth within. She grabbed a thick hand and pulled. The bartender gasped as his head ascended from the bio-prison. His other arm became free, and he shoved himself out of Heidi's stomach and lay on the bar floor. His breath was coming fast and shallow. Joyce got back onto the stage. Her body was festooned with ichor. She danced. The volume of the song increased by the second. She felt the bass reverberating through her whole body. Heidi rolled onto her side and tried closing her stomach, but it fastened crooked like a faulty Levi's zipper. The bartender sat up, rubbing his temples and crying. The song ended, but Joyce kept dancing. Her feet were so light on the stage that she seemed to float. She went to the stripper pole and put her forehead against it, relishing the metallic coolness. She thought about how much she hated that fucking Honda. And how she hated her fucking father. And how she hated her fucking mother. She tried to hate herself but couldn't.

She just couldn't do it.

Afterword

I would like to thank everyone involved in the creation of this book. Nick Clements, proofreader/editor, Matt Clarke, publisher/editor, all of the Beta readers, Corrina Morse, Andrea Tucker, Kevin J. Kennedy, Mike Rankin, Diana Richie, AJ Spencer, Shawn Langhans, Lindsay Crook, Margaret Hamnet, and Reek Feel.

About the Author

Justin Hunter is an author from Missouri, USA. Justin writes for every genre and his work has been published from Morbidbooks to Chicken Soup for the Soul. He loves cross stitching, pipe tobacco, and screen-printed occult candles. His bizarro influences include Garrett Cook, Danger Slater, and Emma Johnson.

Other titles from Planet Bizarro

Peculiar Monstrosities – A Bizarre Horror Anthology
A stripper's boyfriend bites off more than he can chew during a hiking trip.
A man looking for love marries a jukebox.
A popular children's character is brought to life, but something isn't quite right.
A shady exchange on a Kaiju cruise leads to catastrophic complications.

Peculiar Monstrosities is packed with fourteen exquisitely crafted stories from new and established authors of Bizarro fiction.

Featuring tales by: Kevin J. Kennedy, Zoltan Komor, Shelly Lyons, Tim Anderson, Tim O'Neal, Gregory L. Norris, Joshua Chaplinsky, Stanley B. Webb, Jackk N. Killington, Kristen Callender, Michael Pollentine, Tony Rauch, Mark Cowling, and Alistair Rey.

Sons of Sorrow
by Matthew A. Clarke

SOME THINGS ARE BETTER LEFT ALONE

Henk has been living a relatively carefree life in the city since fleeing the horrors of the town of Sorrow with his brother, Dave. Never would he have dreamt of returning. Not even for her.

But time and banality have a funny way of eroding the memory of even the worst experiences, bringing only the better times to the forefront of recall, so when he receives a wedding invitation from the third part of their old monster-fighting trio, he finds himself unable to turn it down.

Sorrow has changed drastically from the place it once was, with the murders and suicides that once plagued the town being used as a selling point by wealthy investors to turn it into a morbid attraction for dark tourists.

Beneath the costumed mascots and smiling families, is all really as it seems? Or by returning, have Henk and Dave inadvertently awoken an ancient evil far deadlier than anything they've faced before?

Sons of Sorrow is the latest bizarre horror from the mind of Matthew A. Clarke.

Porn Land

By Kevin Shamel

OH, NO, PORN IS ILLEGAL!

That's right. Porn stars are criminals, pornographic websites are being systematically destroyed, and not even softcore or selfies are okay. And that's just in our world. It's literally destroying the magick city of sexual expression—PORN LAND!

Phil and Zed, arriving through magickal means and ill-equipped for adventure, must travel through the erotic metropolis and gather pieces of THE PORNOMICRON—a sexual spell-book that bridges our worlds. And it won't be easy. They'll have to get past a giant geisha and her samurai army, a determined detective who's after their asses, a badass dominatrix and her gang, a bunch more sexy people, a bunch of unsexy people... And even more things that will freak you out and make you horny—like a sperm monster and ambulance sex. Will Phil and Zed put the book together, save Porn Land and their new friends, *and* make pornography legal in our world again? (Yes. It'd be a stupid story if they didn't. But it's *how* they do it that you'll want to read about.)

It's a story about sucking, *and* not sucking. It's got hardcore sex *and* a hardcore message. It's ridiculous *and* you'll wanna rub one out to it. It's freakin' PORN LAND, BABY!

Weird Fauna of the Multiverse

A trio of novellas by Leo X. Robertson

— A gimp becomes mesmerized by the koala at a zoo on Venus. She draws him into the battle between the purebred animal supremacy of the park's hippo owner and the anti-establishmentarian koala uprising.

— In a godless future, a rich Martian traveler hunts the former Vatican–now a hotspot for sex tourism—for his deceased wife. When he discovers a dead priest in the streets, he begins to investigate the weird plot of the city's head cyberpope.

— Supercats spend their days responding to rescue calls across their city. Since there aren't enough rescues to go around, one supercat decides to do something drastic and devious to resolve this crisis, changing the industry forever.

The stories of *Weird Fauna of the Multiverse* explore what happens to love and work when pushed beyond the boundaries of human decency.

A Quaint New England Town

by Gregory L. Norris

When Ezra Wilson took the job as a census worker, he never imagined it would lead to a place like his latest assignment. From the moment he turns off the interstate and travels past the village limits, it becomes clear that Heritage isn't just some quaint New England town.

A sinister encounter at an automobile graveyard is only the start. In Heritage Proper, a town divided down the middle both politically and literally, Ezra is met with hostility on both sides of an imposing brick wall that separates warring factions that have maintained a fragile peace. After scaling the wall into Heritage North, Ezra discovers a beautiful young woman held prisoner in a fortified basement room and promises to help her. To do so will expose the last of the small town's dark secrets and lay bare big planetary dangers if Ezra survives his visit to a destination where even the white picket fences are not at all what they appear to be.

Russells in Time

by Kevin Shamel

Because you can never have enough Shamel! In this novella, a trio of recognizable characters find themselves travelling back in time and in the middle of a heated battle between the dinosaurs and a race of giant land-squid. Who will they side with? And will we get to see Russell Brand kicking ass in an Iron Man-esque suit? (Spoiler — yes. We totally will.)

Selleck's 'Stache is Missing!

by Charles Chadwick

Celebrated Hollywood star Tom Selleck has it all: talent, good looks, a winning personality, and a track record of television and movie hits, enjoyed by millions around the world. Until one day, while filming his latest project, an old rival attacks him and steals his mustache. Now, lost and adrift, Tom struggles with his new life. Along with a group of dedicated crew members, celebrity friends, government agents, and the robot voice of an old co-star, he has to find the strength to take on his greatest role ever: tracking down his old rival, retrieving his legacy, and saving the world.

Songs About My Father's Crotch

by Dustin Reade

A collection of bizarre tales from the author of *Bad Hotel*. There's something for everyone in this one. Yes, even you.

The Secret Sex Lives of Ghosts

by Dustin Reade

Thomas Johansson can see ghosts after a near death experience, and has made a living killing them for a second time. After discovering that being possessed by a ghost causes an intense hallucinogenic effect, he goes into business with a perverted dead man named Jerry, selling possession as a street drug (street name: Ghost). But is the farmhouse he sees while possessed really a hallucination? Or is it some else?

The Falling Crystal Palace
by Carl Fuerst

Alice in Wonderland meets Inception in this mind-melting tale that will have you chasing your tail until the final page. This is the kind of book you'll read once, then want to immediately start again.

CPSIA information can be obtained
at www.ICGtesting.com
Printed in the USA
BVHW082355091022
648972BV00004B/148